### "Put your left leg in th

It was easy enough to put all her weight on her uninjured ankle to poke her foot through the loop, but JJ had no choice but to hold on to Ben's shoulder when she needed to lift the other foot. She could feel her cheeks reddening even before he began to slide the loops up her thighs.

"I can do that."

"Take them right up. High as you can. They're elasticized, so they shouldn't be either too tight or too loose." Ben straightened up to take the ends of the waistband and thread a strap through the central buckle. He pulled it tight but then put a fingertip beneath the belt and ran it across her belly.

Dear Lord…that sensation in JJ's gut felt like a trail of small flames.

"Most important thing is to make sure that this band sits over the top of your hip bones," Ben said. "That way, you'll still be safe even if you get tipped upside down."

JJ already felt as if something was being tipped upside down. She didn't dare look directly at Ben…

Dear Reader,

It's always a treat to spend time enjoying the special things in your life, isn't it?

Special people, of course, and places that are special for whatever reason. I had a wonderful weekend recently where I was able to do both at the same time—staying with friends in Central Otago, which has been a favorite part of New Zealand for me since I spent so many summer holidays there as I grew up.

Coincidentally, I was already revisiting the town and small rural hospital I had placed in Central Otago for a previous book—*Melting the Trauma Doc's Heart*—because I remembered a character in that story and it felt like Ben, the paramedic, needed a story of his own.

Joy Hamilton has taken the locum position because she's trying to prove to herself that she's not as boring as other people seem to think she is. It's not a great start when she runs over a sheep that happens to be on the road, sprains her ankle and manages to annoy the gorgeous local paramedic. Things can only get better, though, surely, and it's certainly not a boring start to this new chapter in her life...

*Alison Roberts* xx

# UNLOCKING THE REBEL'S HEART

———

ALISON ROBERTS

HARLEQUIN

MEDICAL
ROMANCE

# HARLEQUIN®
## MEDICAL
## ROMANCE™

Recycling programs
for this product may
not exist in your area.

ISBN-13: 978-1-335-40448-0

Unlocking the Rebel's Heart

Copyright © 2021 by Alison Roberts

This edition published by arrangement with Harlequin Books S.A.

For questions and comments about the quality of this book,
please contact us at CustomerService@Harlequin.com.

Harlequin Enterprises ULC
22 Adelaide St. West, 40th Floor
Toronto, Ontario M5H 4E3, Canada
www.Harlequin.com

**Printed in U.S.A.**

**Alison Roberts** is a New Zealander, currently lucky enough to be living in the South of France. She is also lucky enough to write for the Harlequin Medical Romance line. A primary school teacher in a former life, she is now a qualified paramedic. She loves to travel and dance, drink champagne, and spend time with her daughter and her friends.

## Books by Alison Roberts

### Harlequin Medical Romance

#### Twins Reunited on the Children's Ward

*A Pup to Rescue Their Hearts*
*A Surgeon with a Secret*

#### Royal Christmas at Seattle General

*Falling for the Secret Prince*

#### Medics, Sisters, Brides

*Awakening the Shy Nurse*
*Saved by Their Miracle Baby*

#### Rescue Docs

*Resisting Her Rescue Doc*
*Pregnant with Her Best Friend's Baby*
*Dr. Right for the Single Mom*

*Melting the Trauma Doc's Heart*
*Single Dad in Her Stocking*
*The Paramedic's Unexpected Hero*

Visit the Author Profile page
at Harlequin.com for more titles.

# CHAPTER ONE

THERE WAS NO way to avoid the collision.

Paramedic Benjamin Marshall might have had quite a few years' experience speeding around the rural roads of Central Otago in New Zealand, sometimes pushing his ambulance to the limits on sharp bends, steep hills or even gravel surfaces if he was on the way to an emergency but this time, there was nothing he could do but slam on his brakes and hope for the best when he came around a blind bend to find a car barely off the road, with its driver's door wide open.

Far worse than the horrible thud and screech of metal being mangled as the front bumper of the ambulance tore the door off the car and shunted the whole vehicle forward was the sight of a pair of flailing arms from a person who'd been standing directly in front of the car. Ben got a blurred impression of a slim body, a rope of long, dark hair and arms that were looking oddly graceful as they swam through the air. Arms that vanished at alarming speed as the body disappeared into the deep ditch of a water race that ran along the side of the road as part of the local farm irrigation system.

The shocking thought that he might have just killed someone was foremost in Ben's mind but he couldn't simply jump out of the ambulance to go and find out. He knew, all too well, what could happen if he didn't take the few seconds needed to do something to protect others. He'd seen it happen before. One accident on top of another that had caused totally avoidable fatalities. Slamming his vehicle into reverse, he hit the switch for the beacons before he began moving, to provide a visual warning for anyone else that might be approaching that blind corner. At least any vehicles coming around the bend from the other direction had more than enough room on the other side of the road. Fortunately, the road on this side was still clear and he was able to stop the ambulance, fast enough to skid in the loose gravel on the verge, in a position that could be seen from a distance and would prevent another accident.

Ben was already running at the same instant his feet hit the ground as he jumped from the driver's seat. Pushing the car further off the road was an urgent task as well, he noted as he ran past it, but that was nowhere near as imperative as finding out if there was someone drowning in that ditch.

'Hey,' he called loudly. 'Where are you? Are you hurt?'

The silence was ominous. The kind of silence you only got on a road like this, surrounded by farmland for endless miles in every direction, framed by an impressive mountain range in the distance that still had heavily snow-covered peaks in this first month of spring. Ben could hear the tremulous bleating of a newborn lamb that was somewhere close. He could also hear what sounded like a loud sniff of someone who... was crying? Or trying not to, perhaps.

Two more strides and he was on the edge of the water race. The water at the bottom wasn't deep enough to completely cover the sheep that was lying in the ditch but its head was certainly under water and probably had been for some time.

'It's *dead*...' The woman hunched on the

edge of the bank rubbed at her nose. 'It was my fault. I killed it.'

'It happens.' Ben crouched in the long grass of the verge beside her. 'The sheep shouldn't have been on the road and it's lucky that you didn't try and swerve which could have put your car into the ditch and killed *you*.' He was looking at her carefully, trying to assess how badly she might have been hurt when she'd been hit by her own car. Or was he making an assumption, here?

'Were you alone in your car?'

She nodded. 'Of course I was.'

Oh? Why was it something that should have been obvious? Was she *always* alone in her car? In her life? Ben blinked away the blip of curiosity.

'Where were you headed?'

It was good to keep her talking. He could see that she wasn't having any trouble breathing. Her colour looked okay and a quick body scan didn't reveal any sign of major blood loss happening. The bottom of her jeans and the ankle boots she was wearing looked soaked, however—as if she'd already been in the ditch to try and help the sheep before climbing out to go back to her car.

Maybe if he'd been a few seconds later,

she would have already driven away from the scene. But he hadn't been later and he couldn't leave this woman to wait until any other help arrived. He still needed assurance that she wasn't injured and that wet clothing meant she was going to need some shelter very soon. The sleeves of the neat fitting jumper were also wet but at least that was woollen and would offer some protection against a breeze that still carried the bite of winter temperatures.

'Cutler's Creek,' she responded. 'I don't think it's that far away.' She turned to look over her shoulder at the crumpled bonnet of the car. At the driver's door that was almost completely detached and was twisted enough to be mostly lying on the grass. She screwed her eyes shut as if she rather not see the evidence of what had just happened. She also let out her breath in an unhappy sigh.

'You're right,' Ben said. 'You're not far away. Not that you'll be going anywhere in that car. Let me check you out and then I'll call for some help.' The relief that he hadn't caused a major injury was wearing off and Ben was starting to feel seriously annoyed that this woman had done something as stupid as creating an obstacle on the road that could have killed someone else. 'Our local cop, Bruce, is a dab hand at sorting stuff like this,' he told her. 'You'd be surprised at how often this kind of thing happens. Especially to tourists.'

'I'm not a tourist.' She had the nerve to sound offended.

'Then maybe you should've known better than to leave your car in the middle of the road.' Ben was quite used to keeping his tone calm no matter how much someone annoyed him. He needed that ability when you couldn't know what else might be going with a patient—like a head injury, perhaps. Or low blood sugar. But this woman didn't look as if her brain function was compromised in any way. She was looking at him as if he was the culprit when it came to doing something stupid. He sucked in a measured breath. 'Nobody coming round that bend had a hope of seeing your car in time to stop safely.'

'I tried to get off the road but I could see there was a ditch. And I had to stop—I'd just *hit* something…'

'And you needed to leave your door wide open as well?'

She looked startled. Ben could see the moment that she realised she'd done something dangerous because she hadn't even thought about any potential repercussions. She looked more than startled, actually. The way her eyes widened and her lips parted made her look horrified.'

'So… Are you injured? Do you have any pain anywhere?'

It only took a blink for her to refocus. 'I'm fine,' she said. 'I don't need checking out.'

'You just got hit by a vehicle.' Ben couldn't resist a verbal nudge. 'Like that sheep.'

'Shunted is a more accurate description. It barely touched me. I just lost my balance and fell into that ditch.' She was looking at the unfortunate sheep again. 'I landed on my feet. I'm fine.'

'I'm a paramedic. It's my job to make sure you're really fine.'

'I'm a doctor,' she flashed back. 'And if I *was* hurt, I could take care of myself.' She was struggling to get to her feet as she spoke and Ben could see her wince in pain as she put weight on her left foot even though she was clearly doing her best not to let it show.

He could also see her face much better now that she had turned. Her eyes were almost as dark as that long braid hanging over her shoulder. So dark, they were making her face look paler. Or maybe that was due to the pain she was obviously in.

'Where's it hurting?'

'It's nothing. Just a bit of a sprain, I expect.'

'You've got X-ray vision, then, Dr...?'

'Hamilton.' The polite response to his query about her name was almost reluctant. 'Joy Hamilton. And you are...?'

'Ben Marshall. Station manager for the local ambulance service.'

She was looking almost disconcerted now which was a bit odd but maybe it was embarrassment instead, as the realisation that she'd done something so stupid was sinking in. Why was she heading for Cutler's Creek anyway? Ben wondered. Was she a friend of one of their local hospital's medical staff?

'You a friend of Liv's?' he asked.

'Who's Liv?'

'Wife of the head of our local hospital, Isaac Cameron. Daughter of the local legend who'd been running the place for decades until Zac arrived. Plastic surgeon. She came from Auckland but if you're on the way to visit her, you're out of luck. She's in Dunedin, what with the baby still being in NICU.'

Dr Hamilton was looking bemused. 'I've never met Liv. Never heard of her.'

'Oh…sorry.' Ben shrugged. 'Guess you look like you belong in a big city.'

She did. Those were obviously designer jeans and expensive boots. She had the points of a white collar sitting neatly on either side of the neckline of her bright red jumper. She looked very neat all over, Ben decided, especially with her hair so tightly plaited. It gave the impression that she belonged somewhere like a library rather than anywhere in a busy hospital. Maybe her doctorate was in something like archaeology. Or philosophy? Not that it was any of his business and besides, he was aware of something else now. He could still hear the bleating of that lamb and the sound was getting louder. Distressed, even.

'I do know Isaac Cameron,' Joy Hamilton said. 'I spoke to him on the phone before I decided to take…' She stopped speaking as she noticed Ben tilting his head, looking for the direction the bleating was coming from. He had to give her credit for the speed with which she cottoned onto exactly what he was thinking.

'Oh…that must have been why that sheep was on the road.' Her brow was suddenly furrowed with deep concern. 'There's a baby here somewhere.'

She turned to start walking along the edge of the ditch. Or rather, limping heavily. It was Ben's turn to frown as he tried to assess how bad that injury to her lower leg might be but then she turned her head to glare at him.

'Why are you just standing there?' she demanded. 'Help me look for it.'

There was a sharp pain in her ankle every time she tried to put weight on it but Joy Hamilton wasn't about to admit it. Not when Ben the paramedic would probably give her another one of those looks that told her she was too stupid to be allowed out of a city.

And maybe she was. She'd murdered a sheep. She hadn't given a thought to any blind bend in the road behind her as she'd slammed on her brakes after that horrible thud and…how could she have been thoughtless enough not to make sure her door was shut properly after she'd jumped out of the car? She *never* did anything without thinking about potential consequences. She was the most careful person on earth, in fact.

How could she not be when she'd been brought up having to atone for the fact that her mother had been the complete opposite? She knew how to tick every box and to never miss any important details, which was exactly what made her so good at her job in emergency medicine.

So far, the only real risk Joy Hamilton had ever taken was to apply for the locum position at a hospital in the middle of nowhere, here in the South Island. She might not come from the country's largest city of Auckland but her hometown was the vibrant capital of the country and, right now, Joy would feel a lot more comfortable walking on an inner city Wellington footpath than pushing through almost knee high grass on the edge of this isolated road.

That pain in her ankle was getting worse every time she stepped on it so it was quite possible that she did have a fracture but she'd been humiliated enough by the expression in this paramedic's eyes when he'd asked whether she had X-ray vision. A patient kind of expression, with just a hint of amusement, as if he was dealing with a naughty child. Or someone with very limited intelligence.

Very blue eyes, she remembered now. So blue, in fact, that she turned her head as if she wanted to check that her memory wasn't playing tricks on her. He was too far behind her to see properly but she took in the spiky brown hair with its streaks of blond that made him look like he spent a lot of time outdoors in the sunshine. If they weren't hundreds of miles away from a beach, she wouldn't be surprised to learn that he was into surfing. Not that she should be remotely interested in what this man's hobbies might be. The realisation that the station manager for the local ambulance service, who already knew she didn't belong here, was an undeniably gorgeous looking man only made this situation worse.

No…what really made it worse was the way he smiled at her as she looked back.

She knew that kind of smile. The gleam she would have seen in his eyes if she'd been any closer. This was the kind of man who revelled in anything unconventional. Created chaos, even, by an inability or lack of desire to follow rules. The kind of man her grandfather had had absolutely no sympathy for when their exploits resulted in damage to property or loss of life or limbs.

*'Should've followed the rules, shouldn't they? They're there for a good reason…'*

The kind of man Joy had known to steer very well clear of for her entire life.

A bad boy…

She was definitely getting closer to the lamb, because the bleating was louder, but she couldn't see where it was in this long grass. Then she heard Ben's voice behind her.

'It's in the ditch. Looks like it's stuck in the mud.'

Sure enough, when Joy stepped closer, she could see the small, woolly creature with its legs sunk into the muddy edge of the shallow creek at the bottom of this ditch. It was looking back at her, with black, button eyes and ears that were far too big for it that stuck out sideways and something just melted inside Joy's chest.

'Oh…you poor wee thing.' She slid down the edge of the bank, taking no notice of the way her new Italian boots were disappearing into the mud. She got hold of the lamb and pulled it clear, holding it in her arms as she turned to get back up the bank.

It was then that she realised her injured ankle was highly unlikely to be able to support her weight enough to climb out of the ditch when she couldn't use her hands to help.

'Here…' She held the lamb up. 'You take it.'

Ben's eyebrows rose enough to let Joy know that he was more than a little surprised by her bossy tone.

'Please…' she muttered as an afterthought.

He was grinning broadly as he took the lamb from her arms. He started to turn away but his head swerved as he heard the cry of pain Joy was unable to stifle as she took her first step to climb the bank. He tucked the lamb under one arm and leaned down to offer her his hand.

She had no choice but to take it because the bank was too steep to try and get out on her hands and knees. They both had muddy hands now, thanks to the lamb, which made their skin slippery so Joy had to hold onto Ben's hand with both of hers even as she felt his fingers curl into a firm grip. It was a big hand. Warm. And strong. So strong, she had the impression he could have hauled her out of that ditch in the blink of an eye but he was taking his time and his movements were considered enough to feel oddly gentle.

She had to stand on one leg when she reached level ground. How embarrassing was this? She was covered in mud and her clothes were damp enough to make her shiver in the cold gusts of wind. Far worse than that, however, was that she was going to have to admit that she hadn't been completely honest earlier. She *was* injured and she was going to have to ask for help.

Except she didn't have to ask for anything. Ben put the lamb down on the ground where it promptly collapsed into the long grass.

'Stay there,' he ordered. 'I'll be back soon.'

Stepping forward, as Joy could feel herself wobbling enough that she was about to lose her balance completely, Ben simply scooped her up into his arms and strode back along the road to where he'd parked his ambulance. If his handhold had felt strong and capable, it was nothing to how it felt being in his arms. Joy was fairly slim but she was tall enough to have never felt petite. Until now…

She'd never been swept off her feet and carried like a child by any man. Ever. Her grandfather had had a bad back and hadn't picked up anything heavy. Her boyfriends would have never considered a move like that because she would never have dated them if they had. She was hating this feeling of being helpless, of course, but Joy had to admit there was a rather different reaction beneath the current of what felt like humiliation. A frisson of…what was it?

*Pleasure...?*

No. That would be unacceptable. It was probably more like relief, perhaps, in that she could temporarily relinquish responsibility and let someone else make decisions and look after her?

Fortunately, the journey was over before such an unwelcome notion could make itself any more pronounced. Ben opened the back doors of the ambulance and flipped the steps down with one hand, climbed inside and put Joy down on a stretcher that had a pristine, white sheet over it.

'Where's it hurting?'

'My ankle.'

'I need to get that boot off. Might need to cut it.'

'*No*...it's brand new.' A hint of something like panic was enough to make her not think about what she was saying. 'You'll ruin the luck.' She ignored his raised eyebrows. 'It's got a zip on the side. Somewhere under that mud. Here... I'll find it.'

'Uh-uh...' Ben pointed to the pillow at the top of the stretcher. 'Lie down. I've got this.' As Joy hesitated he gave her a stern look. 'My truck, my rules,' he said.

And there it was again. An invitation to

let someone else look after her and…it was irresistible this time. Joy sank back against the pillow with a shiver, pulled the blanket Ben draped over her up to her shoulders and let him open the zips and ease the boots free from her feet. Her uninjured foot first but she knew he was doing that because it was important, whenever possible, to compare any injured body part with a normal side. It was ridiculous to know that her cheeks were going red because it felt as if she was being undressed for something other than a medical examination.

At least the pain of her injured ankle, especially as he peeled off the damp sock, put this experience firmly back into a professional realm. She could even ignore the extraordinary warmth of his hands against her chilled skin.

'I can't see any obvious deformity,' he told her. 'You've got a good pedal pulse and capillary refill. Can you wiggle your toes?'

She could.

He held her leg with one hand and her foot with the other, putting pressure on in different directions.

'Does this hurt?'

'Yes.'

'How about this?'

*'Ouch...'*

'Sorry. You've got some bruising coming out already there. I don't think you've broken anything but we won't know until you have an X-ray.' A twitch of his lips suggested that he was tempted but had decided against making a comment about her visual abilities again. 'I'll put a compression bandage on this, elevate it and then take you into Cutler's Creek emergency department.'

With a groan of defeat, Joy closed her eyes. This *so* wasn't the way she had intended arriving at her new position. Then her eyes snapped open again.

'You're not just going to leave that lamb all by itself, are you? With its dead mother in the ditch?'

Ben shook his head. 'Don't worry,' he said. He had ripped off the plastic covering of a crepe bandage and he held the end of it against her ankle as he started unrolling. 'It's all under control. I sent Bruce a message before we went on that lamb hunt.'

'Bruce the...policeman?'

'That's the one.' The bandaging that was happening was well practised and swift. It was also firm enough to already be reducing the pain Joy was aware of.

'What did you mean before?' Ben's tone was casual, as if he was just trying to make conversation while he worked. 'About ruining the luck if I'd cut your boot off?'

Okay…this was embarrassing but he was going to find out before long anyway.

'I always get new shoes for a new job. For luck…'

There was a sharp focus in those blue eyes as they flicked up to meet hers.

'You're heading to Cutler's Creek for a new job? As in…the locum that Zac's been trying to find?'

'That's the one.' It was only after she'd spoken that Joy realised she was echoing both the words and tone of what Ben had just said about Bruce the policeman.

He was silent now, however, as he hooked the crocodile clips in place to fasten the bandage and then ease a pillow under her foot and ankle. It felt as if he didn't know quite what to say about the fact that they would quite possibly be working together in the very near future. Because he wasn't exactly thrilled by the idea?

'Wonder what's holding Bruce up…?' Ben

straightened and then turned to peer through one of the small, square windows in the back doors. 'Ah...about time.' He opened the door and raised his voice as he jumped out. 'What took you so long, mate?'

Joy could hear the response.

'I was trying to find someone at home with a tractor who could tow this car off the road. Greg'll be here in a minute but he's not exactly thrilled about cleaning up after another tourist.'

'Ah...' Ben poked his head through the door before pulling it closed and Joy could swear he actually winked at her. 'Be back in a minute,' he told her cheerfully. 'Don't go anywhere.'

As if she could. Joy closed her eyes again and tried to remember why it had seemed a good idea to apply for this new job. Oh, yeah...she'd been fed up, hadn't she? Sick of herself and bemused by yet another relationship disaster which had to win the prize for being the most humiliating.

She was the one who ended relationships—usually because they had become so predictable and unexciting they could only be described as boring—but this time *she* was the one who'd been dumped. By Ian, one of the radiologists in her emergency department, in favour of a ditzy, blonde nurse who was probably ten years younger than Joy. He'd been apologetic when he'd ended things. Kind, even, but his words still rankled.

*'You're a lovely woman, Joy. Gorgeous and smart and damn good at your job. But... you've got zero spontaneity. I don't think you've ever taken a risk in your entire life, have you? I'm sorry, but do you even have any idea how...how boring that can get?'*

Watching the two of them making eyes at each other when they had all been on the same shift had sparked the disturbing thought that there were aspects of life that were passing Joy by. That, perhaps, she might never actually experience?

Her colleagues had been so astonished when she'd announced she was taking leave because she needed a change of scene that Joy had to wonder if they all thought the same as Ian—that *she* was the most boring person on earth. Had Ian been right? Was she the reason her relationships had always fizzled out?

Well...they wouldn't think she was that boring now, would they? She was creating havoc even before she'd stepped through the door of her new job. So much for those lucky new boots. Her car was written off, she might have broken her ankle, there was a dead sheep that someone would have to deal with and...

And she didn't need to recall that cute little face of an orphaned lamb because the back doors of the ambulance opened again and there it was, peeping out from the crook of Ben's elbow, with its long, skinny legs trailing below.

'Can't leave him for Greg to take back to the farmhouse.' Ben used his free hand to scratch the lamb between those ridiculously large ears. 'Poor little guy seems to have broken its leg.'

The lamb bleated loudly as if to agree. There was something about this tall, capable man holding a vulnerable baby creature that was doing something odd to Joy's gut. Something she wasn't sure she particularly liked because it was rather too distracting but it was impossible to look away.

'X-ray vision, huh?'

Oh, yeah...his eyes were an extraordinary kind of blue. And there was a gleam in their depths that suggested that, even if he might think she was somewhat stupid, he didn't think she was the most boring person on earth. Deep down, Joy had to admit she kind of liked that. It even occurred to her that, seeing as nobody here knew anything about her, she could choose to become a totally different person. And create a completely new, exciting kind of life to go along with that new personality?

'Here, hold onto him.' Ben shoved the lamb at her so Joy had no choice but to take hold of it in her arms. 'I need to find something to use as a splint.'

He was bandaging some folded cardboard around the lamb's front leg a minute or two later when the ambulance doors were opened again. A large man leaned in and put something on the floor.

'Here's the doc's handbag,' he told Ben. 'Thought she might need her phone and whatnot. I'll get her suitcases out before the car gets towed and bring them in to the hospital.' He caught Joy's gaze then, and smiled at her.

'Welcome to Cutler's Creek,' he said.

Ben's gaze flicked up to meet hers and she could see that he was very well aware of just

how much she thought her lucky new foot-
wear had failed to do its job.

'Yeah…' He seemed to be trying not to
laugh. 'Welcome to Cutler's Creek, Dr Hamilton. You're going to love it here.'

# CHAPTER TWO

'So…HERE IT IS.' Joy's new boss, Zac Cameron, was smiling as he pulled off the road to park in front of an ancient barn. He gestured towards the small cottage to one side. 'I have very fond memories of living here myself, so I really hope you like it.'

Joy took in the cute weatherboard house with a red, corrugated iron roof and a chimney that meant it had a fireplace. There was a garden bordered by a tall, green hedge between the cottage and barn, an uninterrupted view of those spectacular mountains that were still well snow-capped at the tail end of winter and she'd already noted the lack of any close neighbours.

'I was looking for a change of scene,' she told Zac. 'And this certainly couldn't be more different than my central city apartment in Wellington.'

Joy was aware of a frisson of something like nervousness as she wondered what it would be like in the middle of the night, knowing that there wasn't a single soul nearby. How was she going to cope with that when she'd often felt so lonely living in a crowded apartment block?

Zac came round the car to open the passenger door. 'Come on in. I'll give you a quick guided tour and then leave you to settle in. How's the ankle feeling?'

'It's actually feeling a lot better. Probably because I know it's not fractured.'

The firm bandage was a help as well, as Joy followed Zac to the back door of the cottage. 'See—I'm not even limping that much now.'

'That's great. Back in the day, we'd probably have given you crutches for a while but it's been proven that a low grade sprain will heal faster with early weight bearing. As long as you don't overdo it, of course.'

He lifted a small garden gnome beside the step to reveal a key. 'Not that there's any need to lock up here but you might feel safer at night.'

Zac opened the door that appeared to lead straight into the kitchen. 'Betty, who runs our hospital kitchen and laundry, got the bed made up and she's stocked your fridge with a few essentials.'

'That's very kind of her.'

'And Jill, who's one of our receptionists and is also Doc Donaldson's wife, has been on the phone and found someone who can lend you a car until you get your insurance sorted and a replacement delivered. They'll drop it off tomorrow morning.'

'Wow...' Joy blinked in surprise. 'If I was doing a locum in a city, I expect I'd be lucky to get a hotel recommendation.'

'Small communities have an amazing ability to come together to deal with a crisis of any kind. On the downside, everybody knows everybody else's business but I wouldn't live anywhere else.'

'It's a bonus having accommodation provided. I think that was what persuaded me to take the job.'

'That was the plan.' Zac's nod was satisfied. 'It's hard enough to get anyone to come to a rural hospital for a locum position, let alone consider it as a permanent proposition. We'll have trouble persuading my father-in-law to retire if I don't find someone else.'

'Oh...'

Joy caught her bottom lip between her teeth and took a moment to look around as Zac opened the fridge, perhaps checking on the supplies Betty had provided? There was a black, pot belly stove inside a brick chimney at the end of the room with what was presumably a rack for drying washing hanging above it, a window above the kitchen sink that framed the view of the mountains, well-used-looking pots hanging under a high shelf and an old wooden table and chairs. Realising that this was the absolute opposite of the sleek, modern kitchen in her apartment made it look even more homely. Welcoming, even, but she had to be honest with her new employer.

'I'm not really thinking in terms of a permanent position,' she confessed. 'As I said— I'm just looking for a change of scene, a bit of time out from both where I live and work. I can't commit to longer than the three months we agreed on last week.'

Zac nodded. 'I understand completely.' He pushed the fridge door closed. 'It's not as if Don has any plans to retire any time soon, anyway. I think he's loving going back to full time, to be honest. But you never know. You might just fall in love with—'

He stopped mid-sentence as the back door opened to reveal a large cardboard box being carried inside. Even though the box was hiding the face of whoever was carrying it at that moment, Joy knew who it was as soon as she saw those arms. Ben might have disappeared as soon as he'd delivered her into the care of the Cutler's Creek Hospital staff but he'd left a lasting impression. It was, in fact, disturbingly easy to conjure up the feeling of what it had been like being held in those arms as she'd been carried back to the ambulance. Of having those damp socks peeled off her feet with such care...

Zac was laughing. '...with country life,' he added, quickly to finish his interrupted sentence. 'Hey, Ben. What's in the box? A housewarming present for our new staff member?'

'Something like that.'

The kitchen felt a whole lot smaller all of a sudden. Ben put the box down beside the pot belly stove and it was then that Joy could see what was inside. Curled up on a bed of straw, with its front leg wrapped in one of those sticky firm elastic bandages, was the orphaned lamb she'd pulled out of that muddy ditch.

'Thought you might like some company,' Ben said. 'And that you might like to be the one to look after it seeing as…well…'

'Seeing as I'm the one who murdered its mother?'

Ben's grin widened. 'Let me get this fire going for you. Feels like it could be a frosty night.'

Was he referring to the weather or her tone of voice? And how on earth was she supposed to know how to look after a newborn lamb? For heaven's sake, Ben knew she was a city girl. Was he doing this to wind her up? Maybe coming here had been a big mistake. And maybe it was that negative thought that made her aware that her ankle was aching again. She pulled out one of the chairs and sat down slowly, all too aware that both men were watching her.

'You should put that foot up,' Ben told her, as he struck a match and held it to the kindling already stacked in the stove. 'Be a good idea to ice it a couple of times a day, too, until the swelling is well down.'

Zac was nodding. 'And remember not to overdo the weight bearing. Avoid any strenuous exercise like running or jumping, even if it is just a mild sprain.'

'No problem there.' Joy's huff of sound was intended to be amused but she didn't dare catch Ben's gaze. 'Jumping isn't something I'm generally known for.'

There was a moment's awkward silence. Perhaps both these men were considering how unsuited Joy was to country life. It was Zac who broke the silence.

'Don't feel bad about any of this.' His smile was sympathetic. 'It's almost a tradition around here to start out with a bit of a bang.'

'What do you mean?'

'The day my wife, Liv, first came to Cutler's Creek, she had a plane crash in a field right beside her. On the same road you had your accident, in fact.'

'Good grief...' Maybe running into a sheep and writing off her car wasn't so bad, after all. 'How many people were involved?'

'Just the pilot.' It was Ben who answered her. 'It was a small plane but it was a pretty exciting case.' He blew into the stove to encourage the flames. 'I still use it as a training exercise for our first responders. Not that I got to do much more than watch the doc and Liv in action.'

'Not true,' Zac put in. 'You were just as

much a part of saving his life as we were. It
*was* a great job, though, wasn't it?'

'It had everything.' Ben stayed crouched
by the stove but turned to grin at Joy. 'A
trapped victim, open fracture with significant blood loss, exploding wreckage, intubation needed and the rescue helicopter called
in to land right beside us.' He sighed happily. 'Yeah…it was a *great* job.' He turned
back to his job of building the fire, reaching
for a larger piece of wood in the basket beside the stove.

It was only then that Joy realised she'd
been holding her breath as he'd been speaking—caught up in a story she could read
between the lines of with that succinct
summary. It occurred to her that the survival of the victim had been a bonus. The
real satisfaction had been the excitement and
adrenaline rush of what sounded like an astonishingly dangerous situation to have been
working in. Exploding wreckage? A chopper
coming in to land right beside you? Joy had
never dealt with anything like that and she
didn't want to, either.

Revelling in danger was another 'bad boy'
trait, wasn't it? Along with the better-known
ones of breaking rules and breaking hearts

and not giving a damn because they were just incurably reckless and overconfident, as well.

Joy had to force herself to drag her gaze away from watching what Ben was doing. What was it about men like this that was so inappropriately attractive to women like herself, who would never dream of breaking anything like hearts or rules? Was it because another one of those traits was being passionate? A lover like no other? Joy blew out a breath, soft enough not to attract attention. Okay…maybe they'd *dream* about it. Just occasionally…

She had a horrible feeling that that was exactly what she might be doing later on tonight. Joy closed her eyes for a long blink, just to make sure that neither of these men could see the slightest hint of what she needed to stop thinking about. Right now.

Helpfully, the lamb bleated loudly at that point. Zac started talking at exactly the same time.

'Speaking of Liv, I need to get going,' he said. 'I'm taking Milly and driving up to Dunedin so she can have a couple of hours with Mummy tonight and I can get a cuddle with the mighty Hugo.'

'The mighty Hugo?' Joy was more than willing to talk about something completely unrelated to the man she was having to fight the urge to stare at again.

'Milly's little brother that decided to arrive too early at twenty-nine weeks.' Zac's smile was such a mixture of happiness and worry and pride that Joy could feel the prickle of tears at the back of her eyes. 'He's a wee fighter and he's doing great but he's pretty much the reason you're here. Life's been chaos with the travelling between here and Dunedin and trying to keep the hospital adequately staffed. Thank goodness Liv's dad has been able to increase his part time hours and fill the gaps.'

He turned to Ben. 'Don will be at the hospital to cover any inpatient concerns and I should be back by midnight. I'm hoping you'll be in town for anything out of hospital—or is it date night tonight?'

*Date* night? It certainly wasn't a surprise to learn that Ben Marshall was not single. It shouldn't have been a disappointment, either, and…it wasn't, Joy told herself firmly. It just meant that she might have to step up to her new responsibilities a little earlier than planned.

But Ben was shaking his head. 'Ingrid's gone back to Germany,' he said. 'I think she got bored with shoving tourists off a bridge.' He caught Joy's expression and he did that ghost of a wink thing, like he had when he'd tried to convey the message that Bruce's comment about tourists wasn't anything to worry about. 'She worked in the bungy jumping business,' he added. 'Great fun and I'd suggest you give it go but you said that jumping isn't your thing, didn't you?'

Unlike his recently departed girlfriend, apparently. Joy ignored the implied unfavourable comparison and focused on Zac.

'I could go back to the hospital,' she offered. 'And be on call?'

Zac shook his head. 'You need to rest,' he told her firmly. 'We can get you up to speed tomorrow and plan a new routine that will take a lot of pressure off all of us.'

The lamb was still bleating. It had managed to get up on its feet and was peering over the edge of the box.

'Yeah, yeah,' Ben said. 'I know.' He was following Zac towards the door. 'I've got the milk powder and bottle stuff from the vet in the truck.' He threw a smile over his shoulder. 'I just wanted to check that you were happy to look after the little guy before I brought in all his luggage.'

He didn't wait for any response from Joy because Zac was calling back to him.

'Can you get hold of Bruce and see what's happened to Joy's bags? She'll need them tonight.'

'I've got them in the truck.' Ben's voice grew fainter. 'Anyone would think I'm a delivery service, not an ambo.'

Joy didn't move from her chair. She couldn't. Not due to any pain in her ankle because that had subsided as soon as she'd taken her weight off it. No…she sat unmoving because she was feeling like a stunned mullet. A fish completely out of water. Here she was, in a tiny, isolated old house, with an orphaned lamb that she had apparently just agreed to look after. And possibly the sexiest man in the world was about to walk back through her door in a matter of seconds and they would be alone. Together. In the middle of nowhere.

If she was that way inclined—which she *wasn't*—it could be the perfect opening scene for a sexual fantasy, couldn't it?

Oh, help… Action of some kind was necessary here. Maybe checking for breaking news would provide some kind of global disaster that would be enough of a distraction. A volcano going off, perhaps. Or an avalanche that had buried dozens of people or an earthquake that was expected to cause a tsunami somewhere. Come to think of it, though, she hadn't heard any 'breaking news' notification signals coming from her phone and a quick glance into her handbag didn't reveal its whereabouts. This was disturbing. Joy never lost anything but was it possible that Bruce the policeman had left something important in her car that was now who knew where?

Another rapid search past packets of tissues, sticking plasters, throat lozenges and a dozen other potentially useful items was fruitless. It was also creating enough anxiety to make Joy upend her bag to spill the contents onto the table. She *needed* her phone. If nothing else, it gave her a sense of connection to the rest of the world and that, in turn, would give her a sense of safety when she was alone in the middle of nowhere with Ben the bad boy paramedic.

The new locum doctor was looking rattled.

Ben raised an eyebrow at the mess on the

kitchen table. Who would have thought that someone who looked like she could well be a neat freak would just empty her bag like that? Not that she was looking so neat right now, mind you. There were streaks of dried mud all over those fancy jeans and that expensively soft looking jumper and even on the collar of her shirt. Wisps of shorter hair had come loose from that long braid, too, to curl around the sides of her face and she had bright, pink spots on her cheeks.

Kind of cute, really, despite the fact that she was nothing like the type of women that Ben was attracted to. No… Ingrid had been a perfect example of his type. Tall, blonde and as much of an adrenaline junkie as he was himself. The trouble with the gorgeous European girls who came to work in the adventure tourism industry here was that they were never around for long. They got homesick or their visas ran out and they went back to the other side of the world. But then again, if he was really honest, that was probably a big part of the attraction in the first place. He knew he had an extremely low boredom threshold.

'Too hot in here?' He put the sack of milk

powder on the floor and a plastic jug, stirrer, bottle and teats on the bench.

'No, it's lovely. Unless it's too warm for the lamb?'

'He'll be loving it. When he's a bit bigger you can put him out in the barn.'

'How often does he need to be fed?'

'The vet reckons he's a couple of days old, judging by how dry the umbilical cord is so that's a good thing. He's had some colostrum from his mum so you shouldn't have to be up every two hours during the night or take him into work with you tomorrow to keep up with the feeds.'

Oh…he liked that he could shock her so easily and the way her eyes widened like that. He wasn't sure why he was deliberately making this out to be a bigger deal than it really was. Maybe because she was so obviously out of her comfort zone being in the country? Feeling guilty, he relented.

'Every four to five hours should be fine.' Ben ripped open the bag of milk powder and found the scoop. 'Use this to measure the powder. Let's see…' He read the instructions on the side of the bag. 'It's two hundred grams per litre of water so that's twenty grams to a hundred mils, which is pretty much what this little guy needs at the moment.' He poured a scoop of powder into the bottle. 'That should do the job. Use a bit of hot water to mix it and then dilute with cold so it's about body temperature.'

'Whose body temperature? Mine or the lamb's? And is that a level scoop or a heaped one?'

'Bit over a level scoop, I guess, but that's okay because I'll put in a bit more water. He might drink a hundred and fifty mils.'

'So it's not an exact science, then.' Joy's brow was furrowed, as if this was an alien concept.

'The instructions are on the pack. You need to be careful not to make the milk too rich or you'll end up with a sick lamb.'

The look she was giving him told him that he was not setting the best example in following instructions but even that was kind of cute. It went with that librarian/school teacher vibe she'd given off right from the start. Ben screwed on a teat, shook the bottle to make sure the powder was all dissolved and then led the way to where the lamb was trying to climb out of the cardboard box. He handed the bottle to Joy.

'Give it a go,' he instructed.

She knelt down and offered the bottle to the lamb. Milk dribbled from the teat and the lamb headbutted the bottle, which she dropped instantly.

'Okay…' Ben crouched beside her, leaned over and scooped the lamb up in one hand. 'You behave,' he said. He held the lamb still and, this time, when Joy put the teat near its mouth, it latched on and began sucking greedily.

'Oh…'

The wide eyes this time weren't from shock. It was more like delight and it made Ben smile. He could remember feeding lambs when he was a kid and getting that kind of pleasure out of it.

'Reckon he needs a name,' he said. 'How 'bout Lamb Chops? Or Christmas Dinner?'

The new look he received was withering but it was impressive just how expressive those dark eyes were.

'Shaun,' he offered next. 'As in, you know, the sheep got shorn?'

He hadn't needed to explain. He'd seen the spark of amusement in her eyes as soon as he'd suggested the name. What was entirely unexpected, however, was the soft peal of laughter. And it was a sound that created a not unfamiliar shaft of sensation deep in his gut.

Good grief…he was *attracted* to this woman?

Nah…it was easy to dismiss the thought as completely ridiculous. Even her name was old-fashioned enough to be unappealing. Hadn't his grandmother had a friend called Joy? Oh, yeah…not a friend exactly but an old woman who'd lived down the road and been the biggest gossip in town. She'd had a bad word to say about everyone, that Joy, and a permanent frown on her face that had made the name a bit of a joke.

'See if you can hold the lamb and feed it at the same time,' he said. 'That way you'll know you'll able to cope on your own. Seeing as…you know… I'm not going to be here in the middle of the night.' He couldn't help giving her a bit of a wink, just to tease her. Or maybe he was trying to antagonise her just enough to prove that he wasn't attracted to her in the least. She didn't give him another look, she just took the lamb from his hands, pulled it against the side of her body and continued the feed without missing a beat.

*So there*… the action said. *You're not needed*…

Fine. 'I'll get your bags out of the truck.' Ben got to his feet. 'It's time I got back to the station.'

He carried the suitcases into the cottage a minute or so later. 'Where would you like these?'

'Just leave them there. I'll sort them later.'

Shaun the lamb had almost finished his feed, his tummy as round as a drum, but Joy was focused on tipping the bottle so he could get the last drops. Ben put the suitcases down beside the table and, as he did so, his gaze landed on the pile of items on the table. There was the usual sort of female stuff, like a lipstick and tissues but a whole lot of foil blister packs, as well.

'You carry a pharmacy in your handbag?'

'I'm supposed to be taking some anti-inflammatories for my ankle. Not that it's any of your business.'

'Fair enough.' But Ben couldn't resist picking up another item. 'Wow…do you need a passport to go between the north and south islands of New Zealand now?'

The wide-eyed look he was getting now was nothing short of alarmed. 'Put that down,' Joy commanded. 'It's private…'

But it was too late. Ben had flipped it

open. 'I'm always hoping to see that someone else's passport photo is worse than mine,'
he told her. 'It never is, of course, but…'

Joy was on her feet now. She practically
dumped Shaun back into his box and moved
swiftly across the kitchen, despite her injured
ankle, to snatch her passport out of his hands.
Ben knew why she was so anxious to get it
away from him and it didn't have anything
to do with a bad photo.

'*Journey?*'

She was silent.

'Journey Joy Hamilton.' Ben shook his
head. 'I'm not surprised that you go by your
middle name, mate. What were your parents
thinking? You're far too young to have been
conceived at Woodstock. Was it Glastonbury?' He was laughing aloud now. 'Or were
they on a retro road trip around Europe in an
old VW Kombi?'

'Something like that,' Joy muttered.
'That's how they got killed—driving off the
side of a cliff in Italy. I only survived because
I was strapped into the baby seat in the back.'

Ben's laughter died instantly. 'Oh, God…
I'm so sorry. I…um…really put my foot in
it there, didn't I?'

Joy had dropped her passport back into her

handbag and now she was scooping up the other items, apart from a phone, and shoving them in, as well.

'Doesn't matter,' she told him. 'It's my fault I've never got round to changing my name by deed poll. I don't even remember them. I was brought up by my father's parents.'

'Really? Well, there you go—we've got something in common.' Ben was desperate to make up for being what felt like a real jerk. 'I got brought up by my grandmother, too. Along with my mother, when she visited. Never knew my dad.'

Joy didn't seem to be impressed by the connection. 'I'd appreciate you not broadcasting my first name around the district.'

'It will be our little secret,' Ben promised. He headed for the door, needing to escape, but then he turned. 'You know what? I'm not even going to call you by your middle name.'

Hopefully, his smile was another apology. 'See you around, JJ.'

# CHAPTER THREE

'YOU BUSY, JOY?'

'Not at all. I've just finished the ward round of all three of our current inpatients and I'm writing up my notes. I think Hannah and the twins are ready for discharge later today. Do you want to see them all again first?'

'I'll drop in to say goodbye and wish them luck but not just yet. We've got a patient coming in by ambulance.' Zac smiled at Joy. 'Thought you might like to test out our newly reorganised emergency department?'

'Oh, absolutely...'

Joy returned the smile, abandoning her notes to follow Zac away from the offices that were in the outpatient department, through Reception and into the more clinical areas of the small hospital. It was pleasing to note that, only a few days since her mishap in the ditch, her still-bandaged ankle was taking her weight safely with no more than moderate discomfort.

It was less pleasing to notice a level of anticipation that she couldn't attribute to testing the major reorganisation in the space they used to treat emergency cases that had taken most of a quiet day yesterday. It wasn't that she would be receiving her first patient who was unwell enough to be coming in by ambulance, either. No…while she might not want to admit it, Joy was really hoping that the paramedic bringing this patient in would be Ben Marshall because she hadn't seen him since he'd left her alone with Shaun the lamb.

Only because she wanted to tell him how well the lamb was doing, of course. Joy was proud of herself for how well she was coping with not only getting used to the strange isolation of living in the country but with the added pressure that went with the responsibility of raising an orphaned lamb and keeping up with the feeding schedule. Shaun was clearly thriving, according to the local vet who'd dropped in to introduce himself a couple of days ago and check on how she was doing. What she was a lot less likely to admit, however, was how the small, woolly creature had surprisingly sneaked into a corner of her heart. Maybe it was the anxious bleating that greeted her as soon as Shaun spotted her arrival beside his box, or the pleasure of holding that bottle until the enthusiastic sucking had emptied it. Or perhaps it was the way that the lamb followed her everywhere, as if she was the most important person in the world, until she put it back in its box.

Still in a reorganising mode after work yesterday, she'd cleaned out one of the stalls in the old barn beside her cottage, covering the cobbled floor with a deep layer of clean straw so that Shaun could move out of her tiny kitchen. This morning, heading to work, she'd noticed a stack of old gates behind the barn and wondered if she could make some sort of pen so that the lamb could have time on the grass, as well. She knew she might need a hand to put that together and who better to ask than the person who'd dumped the lamb in her lap in the first place?

It wasn't just an excuse to spend some more time with Ben.

Or was it?

Oh, my... To her consternation, Joy could actually feel her cheeks warming up enough that they would be noticeably pink for some time. Hopefully, the colour would be attributed to her focus on performing well in her new job and not embarrassment that she might have been having some rather explicit and totally inappropriate thoughts about Ben Marshall late at night when a little distraction was needed to prevent the quietness of her solitude dialling itself up from strange to scary.

It would be a good thing if it *was* Ben bringing this patient in. Seeing the real man instead of the fantasy version would probably clear her head instantly. And remind her of why someone like him was absolutely the last kind of man she would want anything to do with in real life. A reality that Joy was not about to let herself get distracted from, especially when she was about to deal with her first emergency case in Cutler's Creek.

They had time to put disposable gowns over their clothes and pull on some gloves before that patient arrived and Joy took pleasure in scanning a room that had been... well...a bit on the chaotic side yesterday. Now there was a logical order and clear labelling to the supplies and equipment and she had to admit she was proud of this, too.

It was a bit of a stretch calling the minor

procedures room an emergency department but it was all that Cutler's Creek community hospital had to deal with serious medical or trauma cases and they had everything they needed, including ultrasound, X-ray, ECG and ventilation equipment. Patients that needed more intensive management could be stabilised and then flown by helicopter or taken by ambulance to a larger centre that had the kind of ED Joy was more familiar with.

Two men came in with an elderly man sitting up on the stretcher and, oh, help… Joy could feel the thump in her chest as her heart skipped a beat and then sped up when she recognised Ben. Seeing those blond streaks in that slightly disreputably tousled hair and, worse, having her gaze met by those astonishingly blue eyes made it actually impossible *not* to think about those small but oddly satisfying fantasies she'd been toying with in the last couple of nights.

Fortunately, the temptation lasted no more than a nanosecond but squashing it so relentlessly probably contributed to her ultra-professional expression that made Ben raise an eyebrow. He turned to his partner.

'Mike…you won't have met our new locum doctor, JJ Hamilton, yet.'

'G'day, JJ,' Mike said. 'I'm one of the firies around here but I help out with ambulance shifts on my days off sometimes.'

'And this is Albert Flewellan, eighty-six years old.' Ben was standing at the head of the stretcher and he had a clipboard, with what looked like a patient report form attached to it, in one hand. 'One of our frequent flyers. A neighbour called us because they hadn't seen him out in his veggie garden for a few days and he didn't answer his door when they knocked. He's got acute exacerbation of his COPD due to a chest infection.' A corner of Ben's mouth quirked. 'He's also forgotten where he put his hearing aids.'

He leaned down and raised his voice. 'You've been feeling a bit short of puff for a few days now, haven't you, Albie?'

Albie lifted the nebuliser mask covering his mouth and nose. 'It's Wednesday today, lad… I think… Could be Thursday, mind…'

This casual handover of a patient was like nothing Joy had ever experienced before. Acute exacerbation of COPD could be serious. If oxygen saturation dropped too low, the patient could need to be intubated and put on a ventilator. He might require a bed in an intensive care unit. Although Albert didn't look in any danger of an immediate respiratory arrest, Joy was still going to follow her normal protocol. To do that, she needed more information.

'What was the oxygen saturation on arrival?' she queried. 'And other vital signs?'

Ben glanced at Mike. 'JJ's down from the big smoke so we'll have to be on our game, here, mate.' He didn't bother looking at the clipboard as he cleared his throat. 'On arrival, we found our patient sitting up in bed.' His tone was formal. 'He had a productive cough and was noticeably short of breath with accessory muscle use and an audible wheeze. Temperature was thirty-eight point one, respiratory rate of thirty-six, blood pressure elevated at one-eighty over one-fifteen, in sinus rhythm but tachycardic at one-ten, two to three words per breath and an oxygen saturation of eighty-eight, which is a bit low, even for Albie.'

The summary was succinct and clear. Joy suspected that, if she asked for the next set of vital signs that should have been taken en route, Ben would be able to recite those from memory, as well.

'Thank you,' was all she said, however, as she unhooked her stethoscope from around her neck. 'Let me just have a listen to your chest before we move you onto the bed, Mr Flewellan.'

'Howdy,' Albie said, pulling his mask clear of his face again. 'Are you new around here…?'

'He's responded well to a short-acting bronchodilator and oxygen,' Ben added. 'His oxygen saturation came up to over ninety within five minutes but we transported him because he usually needs a few days' monitoring until the antibiotics and a course of corticosteroids kick in.'

Zac wasn't looking too concerned that a paramedic was outlining a treatment plan for a potential inpatient. He was, in fact, looking rather intently at Joy.

'JJ?' He asked. 'Is that what you prefer to be called, Joy?'

Listening to the wheeze and crackle in the elderly man's lungs gave Joy a perfect excuse not to respond. She didn't want to respond because…actually, yes…she rather liked this new idea of being called by her initials. It seemed kind of cool. Not something a boring sort of person would prefer. She could also feel her heart sinking. Would Ben remember his promise not to broadcast her unusual first name?

'I suspect it was my idea,' Ben told Zac. 'I've got history with someone called Joy and you know how you can be put off a name? Long story. I'll bore you with it some other time.'

Zac just gave his head a small shake, dismissing the distraction as he saw Joy finish her initial assessment of their patient's breathing. 'Want him on the bed now, JJ?'

A nod was all it took. For both her patient to be transferred and apparently for her new name to be established. Which was fine. New life, new name. Why not? At least all personal distractions were now over and done with and she could focus completely on the job at hand.

She watched as Ben and Mike settled Albie on the bed. Ben raised the end and used an extra pillow as more support to make the task of breathing easier. His movements were swift and efficient as he changed the ECG monitor leads and blood pressure cuff.

'We'll need a chest X-ray to rule out pneumonia, pneumothorax or a pleural effusion,'

JJ said crisply. 'Is there any history of congestive heart failure or cardiac arrhythmia?'

'He's on an ACE inhibitor and a diuretic to manage a bit of right heart failure and hypertension,' Zac responded. 'I'll dig out his file for you but, generally, Albie keeps pretty well between episodes like this. Last one was right at the start of winter so it's a few months ago now.'

'You don't need us to hang around any longer, do you?' Ben handed Zac the patient report form but it was Joy he smiled at. 'Unless there's something I can do to help?'

Oh…that smile… For another nanosecond, it was all JJ could think about. Instant warmth, that's what it was. Like sunshine… Fortunately, it only took a single blink to dismiss the distraction. She didn't do distraction when she had a patient to focus on. And she certainly wasn't going to smile back.

'For future reference, I can recommend Ben as a physician's assistant any time you find yourself short-staffed,' Zac told her. 'As far as any emergency intervention goes, you'll find his skills are as good as any colleagues you've had in an ED.'

That was some recommendation and JJ acknowledged it with a nod and just the briefest flick of eye contact. God forbid that it might be taken as encouragement to smile at her again. She could feel herself straightening her spine at the same time. She needed to assert her own place here as well and she was more than comfortable being in charge of a situation such as this.

'I think we could change Mr Flewellan to nasal cannula until he needs another dose of a bronchodilator. He'll be more comfortable breathing that way with a flow of two to four litres per minute.'

'Sure…' Ben turned and walked towards the bench at the side of the room. Then he stopped abruptly. 'Where's the box gone?'

'You'll find them in the Airway cupboard right in front of you. Top shelf, along with other types of masks. You'll also find they're all labelled.' JJ felt another flash of that pride in her achievement of making this area so much more streamlined. In another moment or so, Ben would probably send an admiring glance in her direction. She could actually feel her response to the expected glance starting already—an even more intense glow of pride because it was Ben Marshall she was impressing?

But Ben's jaw actually dropped as he

opened the cupboard and scanned the shelves.
He looked up to exchange an incredulous
glance with Mike, who was folding blankets
to put back on the stretcher, and then one with
Zac, who simply shrugged and then smiled.

'We'll get used to it,' he said. 'And, I have
to say, it all looks a lot more efficient. Almost
like a small version of a real ED instead of
a minor procedures room trying to be one.'

'Won't be efficient if you can't find something you need in a hurry,' Ben muttered.
'What if we need a cricothyroidotomy kit
urgently after a failed intubation?'

'You'll find it in the next cupboard.' JJ's
calm tone gave no hint of the disappointment of her not inconsiderable efforts being
unappreciated. But then again, this was a
good thing. Her hope that replacing a fantasy
version of the man with the real one would
spell the end of this slightly awkward tension
between them was going better than she'd
hoped. Clearly, he was not only the sort of
man she would never go near on a personal
basis, he had a few shortcomings in the professional department, as well.

'The one labelled "Breathing",' she added.
'Middle shelf, along with the chest drain and
tracheostomy kits. Circulation supplies like

IV kits, syringes, IV fluids are in the next cupboard. It's all organised along the ABC guidelines for primary and secondary surveys that I'm sure you're very familiar with.' JJ knew that the comment was a little condescending but…okay…she was a little annoyed. 'Take a few minutes sometime and you'll see it should be intuitive and easy to find whatever you're looking for.'

'Right…' The syllable was drawn out, which gave it a distinctly dubious note that was even more annoying but Ben found a set of nasal cannula and put them on Albie, gently inserting the prongs into his nose and adjusting the loop to fit securely around his ears. 'You're in expert hands, Albie,' he told him loudly. 'But you'd better make sure you behave yourself.'

Albie seemed to have heard that because he gave Ben a thumbs up signal as he went to help Mike with the stretcher. But then he started coughing and by the time JJ had checked that the figures on the monitor weren't showing a sudden deterioration in his condition and glanced towards the door, Ben had gone. Without any kind of farewell and leaving the unmistakable impression in his wake that he wasn't too thrilled with the changes she'd made here. Or her personality?

Not that she was bothered. It was, in fact, a bonus to add a low level of rudeness to the faults Ben Marshall had already revealed. That she had a mental list of these faults she was only too happy to add to was a bit concerning but she could deal with that without letting it interfere with her new life.

She wasn't going to let anything about the local head paramedic—or possibly the only qualified paramedic in the district—bother her at all.

He had to admit it was bothering him.

For some inexplicable reason, Ben was finding himself thinking about the new doctor in Cutler's Creek far more often than he could find a reason for. Like right now, when he was speeding towards an emergency callout.

She was annoying, that's what it was. A little too neat and tidy, Too organised. Good grief...who labelled spaces on shelves for different types of oxygen masks when you could see what they were through their clear plastic wrapping? Or maybe, if Ben was really honest, the most annoying thing about

JJ Hamilton was that she found *him* annoying but she was so determined not to let him get under her skin. She hadn't batted an eyelash at him refusing to use her real name and she'd taken on the challenge of raising that orphaned lamb even though it had to have been a considerable extra stress on top of getting to know a new town and hospital and sorting out a new car.

According to Greg, the local vet Ben and Mike had met at the pub last night, JJ was doing a great job with that lamb that was now living happily in her barn and putting weight on fast. She'd sorted out the insurance on her car in record time and had even made a good choice for a rural vehicle of an SUV with four-wheel drive capabilities. She'd sorted out old Albie Flewellan, as well, and he'd been discharged from hospital with his medications altered and a home oxygen supply available.

Albie, who'd also been back on his favourite bar stool at the pub last night, thought the new doc was the best thing since sliced bread but, for Ben, she gave him the sensation of an itchy patch that you couldn't quite reach and, what was most annoying was that she popped into his head at the strangest

moments, like when he saw some new lambs
in a paddock as he drove by, or—like now—
when he was nearing the scene of an MVA
and considering where to stop his ambulance
so that it would protect the emergency service personnel as they assessed, treated and
transported any victims.

It was only to be expected that he'd be
thinking about one of the local doctors, of
course, because he was almost surprised not
to find Zac or Doc Donaldson or perhaps
even JJ there already. This was a priority
one callout, which implied that it could be
a critical traumatic or medical incident, and
the scene was a little closer to the hospital
than the ambulance and fire station. The information about the call and its designation
as critical would have been sent through to
the doctors' phones at the same time he'd
been paged.

Not that it mattered that they weren't here.
There would soon be more than just himself
and his volunteer, first responder colleague,
Chris. Bruce was on his way from the police station and they knew Mike was not far
behind them, bringing the fire engine and
extra volunteers. The initial call about this
accident had given them the information that

there was someone trapped in the wreckage so the equipment carried on the fire truck that could cut a car into pieces and release the victim could well be vital. Whether additional resources, such as a rescue helicopter, were required was something Ben knew he needed to assess as soon as possible after arrival so it was disturbing to have something else trying to grab some of his attention.

There was another—just as valid—reason that JJ had crossed his mind, however, so the fact that Ben could see her in his mind's eye so damned clearly really wasn't something to be too disturbed about. Like the accident that had written off her car, this was a single vehicle incident, but instead of being on the side of the road, the driver had clearly caught the gravel edge at high speed, gone out of control and flipped, taking out the barbed wire fence and a couple of posts before continuing to roll more than once, by the look of it, to end up on its roof well inside the paddock's boundary.

The only car on the roadside was the person who'd stopped and made the call to the emergency services and, sensibly, had their hazard lights flashing. Rolling down his window, Ben thanked the middle-aged woman and asked if she could stay long enough to be confirmation for the next vehicles that they were on scene. Then he glanced at Chris.

'There should be a gate further down this road. I'd rather drive in so that we've got all our gear handy.'

'I can see it. At the end of that macro-carpa shelter belt between the paddocks.' Chris reached for the radio. 'I'll let Mike know where we are.'

Ben could hear Chris confirming that they'd located the scene but his mind was racing in another direction. Not yet on what he might find in the overturned vehicle but he knew that focus would come the moment he got through the gate and into the paddock.

No...dammit, it was JJ Hamilton he was thinking about. Again. She could have hit the gravel like the driver who'd crashed here if she'd swerved too hard to avoid that sheep. Her car could have been flipped if he'd come round that bend and hit the back of it full on instead of just collecting the door and ripping it off. Ben could see that moment of impact in his mind's eye, like a movie flashback. He could see JJ's body fully airborne and the re-lief of finding her conscious and relatively unhurt only seconds later.

Oddly, he could also remember that blip of curiosity that went beyond a normal assessment of a potentially injured person. Like how he'd wondered why she'd made it sound as if she was always alone. He could also remember the surprise of his eyes meeting hers that very first time. Because they were so dark? Or was it something more significant, like recognising that she was about to become an annoying presence in his life?

He had a few more seconds as Chris got out of the ambulance and wrestled to pull an old, wire gate through long grass far enough for the ambulance to get into the paddock. His brain was determined to use that tiny amount of time to let one more thought morph with a new one with lightning fast speed—as if it was determined to solve an irritating puzzle by joining the dots in a mental image.

JJ's eyes. How dark they were. The way they'd lit up with delight when she'd been feeding Shaun the lamb that first time. The way it had made him smile. And tease her about a name for the lamb.

The shock of thinking it was possible he was attracted to her.

It felt good to put his foot on the accelerator and bump the ambulance over old tractor ruts in the ground. He was shaking off unwelcome thoughts at the same time.

Of course he wasn't attracted to JJ. Or, if he had been for a nanosecond or two, their last encounter had been more than enough to make any attraction sink as fast as a lead balloon. He liked his women to embrace adventure and the adrenaline rush of the unexpected—just like he did himself. It was obvious that Dr Hamilton compartmentalised her entire life and then probably put labels on the boxes.

And, if that wasn't enough in itself, her real name was Joy, and that reminded him of his grandmother's patience with the old gossip down the road. And that only made him remember his grandmother and feel the ache of loss that the only person who had ever truly loved him was long gone.

It was always best not to think about anything that could pull you down like that and Ben had learned just how to banish thoughts effectively enough to make sure they weren't going to reappear in a hurry. You just needed to keep busy. Keep moving. To embrace any new adventure and that included women, of course. Maybe that annoying niggle he was so aware of was there because he hadn't done anything to fill the gap that Ingrid's departure had left in his life?

Bit of a shame the locum doctor was so not his type. And that she found him so annoying. No chance to get bored or have someone wanting more than he was prepared to offer when they were only in town for a month or three.

He stopped the ambulance just long enough for Chris to clamber back in and then they were off across the paddock. Heading for the unexpected and a potentially challenging job. Ben could feel his adrenaline levels climbing as he prepared for that challenge and he was now completely focused on the only thing that mattered. Throwing himself into a new challenge.

Finding out whether the unfortunate driver of this car was still alive. And then doing whatever it took to keep him that way.

# CHAPTER FOUR

AMAZINGLY, THE DRIVER was more than simply alive. He was conscious and alert.

'What's your name?' Ben asked, after introducing himself through the shattered window. While he could see that the young man was upside down and clearly uncomfortable with his head pressed onto the back of a mangled seat, amongst deflated airbags, he was breathing reasonably well and looked alert enough for Ben to think there might be no need to summon backup with extra skills and equipment to deal with critical injuries.

'Nathan.'

'Does it hurt when you breathe?' Reaching through the window, Ben put his fingers on Nathan's wrist, to feel for his heart rate and rhythm.

'Nah…it's all good…'

'Were you knocked out?'

'Dunno…'

'Can you remember what happened?'

'Guess so…it was all a bit quick.'

'Anything else hurting?'

'My leg, man… I can't move it.'

Ben shone his torch up into the interior of the vehicle, to the floor that was currently the roof. 'That's because it's caught under the dash.' The light caught a blood stain on Nathan's jeans but, again, it didn't look enough of an ongoing blood loss to be alarming. 'We're going to need some help from the firies to get you out of here, mate.' He looked over his shoulder to see the fire truck currently negotiating its way past the larger rocks in this paddock.

Nathan groaned. 'I've wrecked my car, haven't I? And I've only…had it for…a week or two.'

The increasing effort of breathing upside down was obvious. So was something else that Ben could smell on the young man's breath.

'You've been drinking, mate?'

'Nah…not since last night. Never…drink and drive…'

Ben caught his Mike's gaze as the older man walked around the car, assessing how they were going to get their patient out. The erroneous notion that you could party hard until the early hours and then get up and be sober enough to drive safely wasn't uncommon.

'You weren't wearing your safety belt, either, were you?'

Nathan closed his eyes. 'I forgot… You're not going to…give me a hard time, are you?'

'Let's get you out of here. You can talk to Bruce about that one later.' Ben unzipped the pack of gear he had beside him. 'We're going to see if we can get a collar on you to protect your neck and then Chris, here, is going to give you an oxygen mask, because it's a bit difficult breathing upside down, isn't it?'

Nathan was groaning again. 'My leg…it's *really* hurting…'

'On a scale of zero to ten, zero being no pain at all and ten being the worst you can imagine, what score would you give it?'

'Eleven…no…*ahh*…make that a twelve.'

'That bad, huh? I'm going to put a line in your arm as soon as I can,' Ben told him. 'And then I can give you something for the pain, okay?'

'Yeah…that'd be good…'

The car jerked as Mike wrenched a door

on the other side of the car. 'I've got this one open enough,' he told Ben. 'Can you work on him from this side while we get that other door off so we can roll that dash back?'

'Sure thing.'

'Right.' Mike turned to the volunteer fire officers he had with him. 'Let's get some chocks in to stabilise the car and then I'll need the spreaders.'

It was more than awkward to squeeze far enough into the car's interior to get a cervical collar onto Nathan and there wasn't enough space to make it simple to get an IV line inserted into his arm. Ben's first attempt to find a vein was unsuccessful. The second failed because, as he started to push the cannula into place, the screech of metal being prised open made Nathan jerk his arm clear.

'Try and hold still for me, mate,' Ben said calmly. 'It's going to be a bit noisy because we have to cut the car up to get you out. Chris, can you give me a dot to cover this and another cannula, please?'

He had to make a third attempt. IV access wasn't important just for the pain relief that Nathan needed. Ben wanted a line available and fluid to keep it open in case his condition deteriorated. He could see the blood stain on the jeans spreading and he had no idea what was happening to the lower part of Nathan's leg that was hidden behind the squashed dashboard. How long it would take to get him clear was also unknown and if there was significant, ongoing blood loss, the longer it took to get venous access the harder it would get as blood pressure dropped and veins shrank.

The team around him might be mostly volunteers rather than paid employees like himself and Mike but these men—and women—were passionate about the contribution they made to their community by keeping the emergency services viable. They took on as much training as they were offered to learn and practise techniques and protocols and Ben was proud of their skills and commitment. The door of this wrecked car was cut free, the crushed dashboard rolled back enough to release Nathan's leg and then as many sets of leather gloved hands that could get close enough got him onto a hard backboard and gently slid him clear of the car and onto the waiting stretcher.

'Hang on…' Ben warned. 'Watch out for the tubing.'

His warning came too late. While he was

holding the bag of IV fluid well out of the way as Nathan was being lifted out, the tubing snagged on a rough piece of metal. While he'd taped the tubing in place, he hadn't had time to put a bandage over it as well and it didn't take much of a jerk to pull the tape off Nathan's arm and then the cannula out of his vein. But the amount of blood that was being lost from that puncture wound was not as much of a concern as the bleeding from their patient's leg that had increased dramatically having been freed from beneath the dashboard. The sheet on the stretcher was getting rapidly soaked and Ben's white shirt had blood smears in several places.

'Put a pressure dot on that arm,' Ben instructed Chris. 'I'll deal with his leg.'

'Can I help?' Mike was right beside him.

Ben was using his shears to cut away what was left of Nathan's jeans on this side. 'I need a large gauze pad,' he told Mike. 'And then a couple of bandages. I'll have to try and control this bleeding with pressure.'

It was just as well he'd had time to give Nathan some IV pain relief because he could feel the crunch of a broken bone as he put enough pressure on the deep cut to stop the blood loss. It was still painful enough to make his patient cry out, however, and there was no quick way to top up the analgesic.

'Do you want the IV roll?' Chris asked, as he put another round, sticky dot over the puncture wound on Nathan's arm. 'To get a new line in?'

Ben wrapped a bandage as tightly as he could to keep pressure on the leg wound.

'No,' he responded. 'Grab a splint. I'll stay in the back and keep an eye out for break-through bleeding but we're close enough to the hospital and it'll be easier to sort everything there.' Ben had to shake away the thought that it would give JJ a chance to show off her newly organised emergency department again.

'Let's load and go,' he told Chris, as soon as he'd secured the splint as well as his pressure bandage.

'I feel sick…' Nathan was looking pale.

It was Mike who reached for a container and a towel but he was too late. He gave Ben a sympathetic glance as they loaded and secured the stretcher in the ambulance.

'Don't breathe too deeply,' he murmured. 'It might put you over the limit.'

Slamming the doors shut as they took off only intensified the smell in the back of the ambulance but it wasn't anything Ben hadn't already dealt with too many times to count. JJ might find it a bit more confronting, he thought as they got closer to Cutler's Creek Hospital. It wasn't as if they had a team of nursing and ancillary staff to deal with messy stuff like this.

To her credit, however, JJ did not appear fazed by either the smell or the appearance of her new patient when they arrived a few minutes later. She watched intently as Ben and Chris transferred Nathan to the bed and listened, just as carefully, to their handover.

'Nathan Brown, twenty-one years old. His car came off the road at speed, rolled and ended up on its roof with Nathan trapped. He had a GCS of fifteen on arrival, probably wasn't KO'd and doesn't appear to have a head injury.' Ben had to pause and take a breath before he listed vital signs that had all, surprisingly, been within normal limits. 'It took approximately twenty-five minutes to get him out,' he finished, as he tucked a pillow beneath Nathan's head. 'He's had five milligrams of morphine for the pain from that fractured tib/fib.'

'How's the pain level now?' JJ asked, stepping closer to Nathan. 'On a scale of zero to ten?'

'Ten,' Nathan told her.

The look Ben received suggested that he hadn't provided enough pain relief for his patient.

'To be fair,' he said, 'Nathan did say it was twelve initially, so it's improved.'

He noticed that JJ was checking the monitor and knew that she would be thinking that the heart rate and general appearance of this patient did not back up his claim that he was in severe pain and, if anything, his blood pressure was lower than might be expected. He also noticed the way her nose wrinkled, just a little, as she took in a new breath.

It was a very subtle admission of how bad Nathan smelled with that combination of stale alcohol and vomit. A tiny, rabbit-like twitch. Cute, Ben found himself thinking instantly, until he realised that this might be another impression of this woman that would pop into his head at unexpected moments and add to that background level of annoyance she was causing. Not that she noticed his frown, because she had turned to the nurse in the room with them, Debbie, who had shears in her hand, ready to cut away the remnants of Nathan's jeans.

'Maybe you could find a gown for Nathan soon? That way we could…ah…dispose of his clothing?'

Her attention was on the monitor again. 'Blood pressure's a bit on the low side of normal,' she murmured. Her next glance was back at the stained sheet of the stretcher but quickly shifted to Ben. 'Estimated blood loss?'

'Hard to say.' Even a small amount of blood could look like a lot when it was spread around and wicked into fabric. 'Less than five hundred mils, I'd guess.'

But Ben was getting another look that he could read only too easily. Strike two for his patient care? Was she thinking she might want to see their SOPS—standard operating procedures—with reference to controlling haemorrhage on scene? Maybe she had no real understanding of how difficult it could be to control external blood loss when you couldn't actually reach the body part that was bleeding? Or when it took time to remove a victim from wreckage so that you could get close enough to do something like put pressure on a laceration?

That look was no more than a brief glance but it also made Ben suddenly aware of how scruffy he must look, as well, with his blood-stained shirt and it was quite likely he didn't smell so great himself. But it went with the job, didn't it? And he knew he did his job damned well. He certainly didn't need someone giving him a school teacherish look that suggested he could have done better. Ben was officially annoyed now but there were no surprises there, were there? This was Dr Journey Joy Hamilton, after all. Big city girl with a dose of prim and proper and an addiction to protocols.

'We did have a patent IV line and fluids up,' he said, keeping his tone perfectly even. 'Unfortunately the line got caught as we were extricating Nathan from the car. I didn't want to hang around to put another one in.'

He didn't need to add that it had taken more than one attempt to get an IV in in the first place. He could see JJ noting the sticky spots covering the puncture sites before she wrapped a tourniquet around his other arm. Her slick insertion of a cannula, the snap of the tourniquet being released and the tape being torn off to secure the new line was impressively efficient but it felt like another judgement of his skills. Even attaching the tubing and the bag of IV fluid was swift and professional. Of course it was. They were in a controlled environment and everything was far simpler—including the availability of the two-way stopcock in the tubing as a painless way to remove a blood sample or inject medications when needed. The way JJ's gaze grazed his as she moved on was really an unnecessary confirmation of that judgement.

*See?* It seemed to say. *This is how it should be done. Easy-peasy...*

'There we go, Nathan. I'm going to top up your pain relief a bit while we have a good look at your leg. If it's anything more than a simple fracture, though, we'll have to transfer you to a bigger hospital.'

She'd have to ask Ben what the protocol was for a transfer like that, JJ realised, because it wasn't something she'd talked about in any detail to Zac yet and he wasn't here today. Ben didn't seem that happy to be here today, either, for some reason. He'd been almost glaring at her as she'd finished setting up the bag of IV fluid. Was he bothered that she was replacing the IV line that had been pulled out?

If so, he needed to get over himself. It wasn't a criticism of his work, she was just getting on with what needed to be done. And one of those things was collecting a blood sample. It was quite obvious that this young man had been drinking heavily and, no doubt, Bruce the local cop would want to know the level of intoxication.

Was he annoyed because he was just standing there and watching her work when he could have been more usefully employed by replacing that IV line himself? His colleague was almost finished tidying up the stretcher so it was quite possible that he would head out the door any moment, perhaps without even saying goodbye again? JJ didn't want that to happen. She was the only doctor in the hospital at the moment and, while she could manage on her own if she had to, she'd would much prefer to have Ben's assistance to take X-rays and organise a patient transfer if it was needed.

At least she could give credit where it was due when she took the pressure bandage off Nathan's leg.

'Great haemorrhage control,' she told him. 'That's a deep laceration and it's not even oozing now.'

'You going to suture it?'

'That'll depend on the X-rays. If surgery's needed, there's no point. We can just get another clean dressing on and make sure it's splinted well enough for transport.' She offered Ben a bit of a smile. 'I'll rely on your expertise for that.'

The quirk of Ben's eyebrow suggested that her attempt to defuse that hint of background tension between them had failed. Maybe a direct appeal would work better.

'Can you stay to help with the X-rays?'

There was no hesitation on Ben's part. If anything, JJ could see a flash of concern in his expression. 'Are you and Debbie on your own at the moment?'

'Yes… I persuaded Don to go with Zac to Dunedin to see Liv and the baby. I assured them both I'd be able to cope with anything.'

'Ah…so that's why you didn't respond to the message about this accident?'

JJ blinked. 'I thought it was just alerting me to an incoming patient. Was I expected to turn up at the scene?'

'Zac always does, if he's not in the middle of something here. Doc Donaldson, too. Especially if I'm not on duty or it's a priority one callout where there's the possibility of critical injuries or illness.'

It felt like Ben was criticising her now, which seemed unfair. 'I *was* in the middle of something, actually. A bit of minor surgery.'

Debbie looked up from her recording of a new set of vital signs for Nathan and grinned at Ben. 'A nail trephination,' she told him. 'Old Harvey White's really got to stop carrying bricks around. He dropped another one on his toe yesterday and he couldn't even walk because of the pain today.'

'No way…' The way Ben smiled back at Debbie and the feeling that they both knew far more than she did about her patient made JJ feel distinctly left out and she felt a pang of something she didn't like. Envy, perhaps, of feeling like she really belonged somewhere like these two seemed to have? Or that connection when things could be said without actually saying anything aloud?

Ben's smile was fading as he turned back to JJ but she could see a gleam of amusement still in his eyes. Was he mocking her because she chosen not to respond to a potentially life-threatening situation outside the hospital in order to drill a hole in a toenail to relieve pain?

'What did you use?' he asked. 'A needle or a paperclip?'

Ignoring the query made her tone a lot crisper than she might have intended. 'Let's get on with these X-rays, shall we?'

The images of the complicated fracture involving both the bones of Nathan's lower leg made it obvious an expert orthopaedic opinion would be needed.

'What's the normal protocol for transferring a patient?' JJ asked, a short time later, as she and Ben both stood looking at the illuminated images with Nathan drowsing on the bed behind them.

'If the patient is status one or two, we call in the air rescue service,' Ben responded. 'The helicopter can land in the hospital grounds. If it's not critical, we transfer by road. Usually we can get an ambulance dispatched from either Dunedin or Invercargill and meet them halfway.' He paused for a moment, his gaze level—as if he was about to impart significant information. 'They're both around three hours' drive from Cutler's Creek so that means our ambulance is unavailable locally for at least ninety minutes.'

JJ nodded. It was obvious that calling a helicopter in to transport Nathan would be a waste of valuable resources but…oh…was he was warning her that she would be responsible for any out-of-hospital emergencies while he was gone?

She was about to tell him that wouldn't be a problem. Zac had showed her where the emergency kit was kept so she could put it into her car now, just in case. She could take the defibrillator from the procedures room when or if she got a call. But it was Ben who spoke again before she had a chance to say anything.

'We've got a backup transport vehicle— our old ambulance. I can call on a volunteer to do the driving. Nathan's stable enough not to need a medical escort.'

JJ stared at him. 'Because you don't think I could cope?'

'Have you ever been out with an ambulance crew?'

'Why should that make a difference? I am an emergency trauma specialist. I'm trained to deal with anything.'

'In a big city ED, sure. Where it's relatively easy to work your way through a flow chart protocol and follow every rule. Or even in a minor procedures set-up like this one that's got everything available and *labelled*.'

Okay…that was a direct jab. But he wasn't finished yet. 'You might find things a bit more challenging if you're trying to put IV lines into upside down people and working in conditions like crawling around inside a wrecked car,' he told her. 'Especially in a rural environment when specialised backup might be too far away to rely on. You might even find that it's not easy to control haemorrhage and your patient might lose a bit more blood than you're happy with.'

Had Ben felt he was being criticised when she'd asked for an estimation of blood loss? Was he also trying to tell her that he didn't think she belonged in Cutler's Creek? Or was he throwing another challenge at her—like leaving her with an orphaned lamb and a sack of milk powder? Not that it mattered, it was just a bit weird how strongly JJ felt she needed to prove herself to this man.

No…maybe it was just that she needed to prove herself, full stop. To demonstrate that she was capable of embracing new challenges. That she didn't fit neatly into some labelled box, perhaps, which could always come across as being unimaginative or dull. Boring, even…

'That's exactly what you *should* do,' Ben concluded.

'What is?'

'Find out. Get out of your comfort zone. Come out on the road with us for the next priority one call or you could just join one of our training sessions in the meantime. If you're up for it, that is.'

Yep. This was a challenge being issued, all right. And JJ was definitely up for it.

'I'm in,' she said. 'For whatever comes first. As long as I'm available, of course.'

He didn't have to say anything. She could see the warning that dealing with something as minor as a painful toenail would not be a legitimate excuse. But there was humour in the look as well and JJ was quite sure he could read her silent acceptance of the message that was also an apology. For a heart-beat, it felt like there was a level of the kind of understanding that formed a palpable connection. That they were about to share a smile. To place the foundation stones of a genuine friendship, even?

Maybe that was disconcerting for them both, which might explain why they both turned away at exactly the same moment.

'Just be prepared for anything,' Ben said.
'You might have to use every bit of that
training of yours.'

## CHAPTER FIVE

HER TRAINING CLEARLY hadn't included anything like this.

And perhaps climbing the foothills of
mountains wasn't something JJ Hamilton had
ever chosen as something she wanted to do
in her time away from work. She looked like
she was struggling with this steep ascent,
that's for sure. She'd been out of breath even
before they'd reached this rugged part of the
track that required some clambering over
large rocks and Ben could see how much
effort it was taking to cling onto a smooth
boulder and haul herself up to the next foot-
hold.

She also looked as if she was going to push
herself as hard as it took, despite the fact she
was still recovering from that sprained ankle
and Ben didn't want to end up with two patients to carry back down the slope. He held

out his hand as she reached further up the
rock, sliding it beneath and curling it around
hers before she had the chance to refuse his
offer of assistance.

Her grip was surprisingly strong as she returned the pressure and it was no hardship
to pull her up to his level. She felt as light as
a feather, in fact, probably because she was
also pushing hard herself with her legs. The
ease and speed with which she arrived beside him was enough to put her unexpectedly
close to Ben. So close that he could feel the
puff of her trying to catch her breath on his
own face and he could clearly read the surprise in dark eyes that were only inches from
his. It had also been so fast that he hadn't
quite let go of her hand yet and, despite the
fact that they were both wearing protective
gloves, he could feel the shape of her hand
and even the warmth of it, as if they both
had bare skin.

It wasn't just warmth. There was a heat
there that had absolutely nothing to do with
body temperature. Shocked, Ben released his
grip on her hand. He had to resist the urge to
rub his own hand on something to try and
get rid of the sensation that now seemed to
be racing up his arm and into the rest of his

body. He was also finding it hard to break that eye contact.

'You good down there?' Mike and other members of the Cutler's Creek mountain search and rescue team were already out of sight above the rocks on this well-known track.

How long had they been standing here like this? Surely not more than a few seconds, but JJ's breathing was a lot less ragged so maybe it had been longer.

Too long…

'Come on…' There was relief to be found in breaking that eye contact. 'We don't want to get left too far behind.' He knew he could speed up now that they'd negotiated the scramble over boulders and there was a good trail to follow. 'I use this Twin Rocks track as both training and a fitness test for anyone who wants to come onboard as an emergency services volunteer,' he explained, as they picked up their pace. 'I've found that the people who get fit enough to do this track easily have what it takes to cope with just about anything that gets thrown at them unexpectedly. Not a good look if I'm last.'

He couldn't help just another quick glance over his shoulder but that was only professional concern. He had to make sure JJ was going to safely manage this last section of the challenging track.

That look of sheer determination in the face of a task that had to be pushing her to her physical limits was actually quite impressive. It didn't really matter if he came in last, did it? The other members of his team would know he was just taking care of the new doctor who'd put her hand up to join this training session.

Ben slowed his steps. Not enough to make it obvious he was trying to make it a bit easier for JJ. He was just adjusting the pace to make sure she didn't collapse or something. He didn't want to break that determination, either, because he knew how important it could be. He also knew that a city girl's level of fitness was unlikely to be honed for an outdoor challenge like this so he turned his head just far enough to offer a half-smile.

'You're doing great,' he muttered.

Doing great?

JJ was dying here. Her face felt like it was on fire, which could explain why her lungs were burning so painfully. Her heart was thumping and she had trickles of perspiration making her back itch. The muscles in her legs were about to give up completely and her ankle, although it was well strapped, was aching more than it had in the week since she'd made that pact to either go on a priority one callout or join one of Ben Marshall's training sessions that Zac had warned her were legendary.

*'You'll certainly see how fit you are,'* he'd said with a grin. *'Unless you die first.'*

And…to add insult to injury, Ben had just done it again—acted like he really, *really* didn't like her. He'd offered her his hand and helped her over a boulder that would probably have been too much for her aching body but then it had been like he'd suddenly noticed it was her hand he was holding and he'd dropped it like it was burning him. He'd been looking at her, too, kind of like after they'd been talking about transferring Nathan with his badly broken leg. When she'd almost believed that there was a real connection between them and that they could end up being good friends.

*Ha…* That wasn't going to happen, was it? The best JJ could hope for was that she could prove she was good enough for these Cutler's Creek locals to give her a chance to feel like she was accepted here. That she could belong. If she wanted to, that is. And maybe that was the crux of this challenge. JJ wanted to prove that she could be whoever she wanted to be. She was only thirty-five years old. Surely she wasn't too old or set in her ways to choose a path that could change her life for the better?

'Hey…' It was Mike the firie who started the applause as JJ and Ben finally caught up with the small group standing under what appeared to be a rather dramatic cliff as they busied themselves getting into harnesses and sorting ropes. 'Go you, Doc. First time is always the hardest.'

JJ had no breath to respond but she couldn't help a smile that felt like the widest she'd ever had. Ear to ear, that's what it was.

Pride…

'So, this is Twin Rocks.' Ben wasn't looking at JJ as he waved an arm towards the cliff but it was clear that she was the only one who needed this information.

'It's really one rock face but it looks like two separate cliffs because of that deep gap in the middle. A hundred and fifty metres of rock wall that's been well set up with permanent bolts to rappel from and varying degrees of difficulty depending on which section you choose.' He still wasn't looking at JJ. 'People come from all over the country to abseil here so it's not that uncommon to get a call to someone who's injured themselves and they may well be stuck on the wall somewhere. That's why just getting here might not be enough to save them.'

He turned to JJ and she could see he was perfectly serious. The huge effort she'd just put into getting this far up the mountain wasn't all that was expected of her.

'Abseiling is a skill we use quite a lot. It might be a climber up here or a car that's gone off the road in the gorge that leads into Cutler's Creek. Sometimes it's not possible to get a chopper in to winch someone down in time so it's up to us. We've got to get to a patient, stabilise them and then carry them out somehow.'

JJ nodded. It made sense. Her respect for what Ben did in his line of work had just gone up too many notches to count. That there were members of the community here prepared to train and then risk their lives to help in difficult rescues was also impressive enough to take her breath away.

'This is just one of our regular training

sessions to keep our skill sets sharp,' Ben continued. 'All these guys have done their basic abseiling training so you've got a bit of catching up to do. Let's take the track that gets us up to the top and then I'll throw a harness on you and you can give it a go.'

This training session for the mountain search and rescue group had been astonishingly challenging so far but it hadn't been terrifying. Until now. Not that she was going to let Ben see how much she wanted to turn around and get back down that track as fast as possible. There had to be an inspirational saying she could benefit from right now. 'No guts, no glory' perhaps? Or 'Feel the fear and do it anyway'?

She could do that.

Maybe...

It was like a point of no return and she was ready to take that step but then she saw the quirk of Ben's lips. A beat later, there was a ripple of laughter through the group.

'That's Ben's little joke,' Mike told her. 'Don't worry. You'll do your abseiling training somewhere else.'

Ben was nodding. 'And it won't be when you're already stuffed from walking five kilometres up a steep hill.'

'I would have given it a go,' JJ said quietly.

'I know.'

Good grief, was that a flash of something like admiration she could see in his eyes?

'What I will ask you to do, if you're up for it, is to be a patient for us. See that ledge up there?' Ben pointed towards an overhang that was only a few metres off ground level. 'We'll set you up with a helmet and a harness and just get you to sit on the ledge. The rest of us will pretend you're actually further up the cliff, go to the top and plan how we're going to get you off the ledge safely, assess your injuries and then get you down the track to where the ambulance will be waiting in that roadside parking area.'

It sounded like JJ could actually be a useful participant in the training session, despite being tired and sore and having probably slowed the session down already, and she was more than willing to play her part.

'What are my injuries going to be?'

'Oh…let's see…' There was another smile hovering around Ben's mouth. 'How 'bout we make it an injured ankle? A bad sprain? No…a fracture.'

'Am I conscious?'

'Yep. You're in a lot a lot of pain and you're

cold. You've been sitting on that ledge for a few hours waiting for help, and the weather's closing in, which is why they couldn't send a chopper to rescue you.'

'Past medical history?'

'You're young,' Ben told her. 'And perfectly healthy.'

'Okay. One more question…'

'Shoot.'

'How do I get up onto that ledge without *really* breaking my ankle?'

'Come with me.' Ben started moving closer to the cliff, turning to speak to Mike as he passed the group. 'Take everybody up the track,' he said, 'and get sorted with your ropes and knots. I'll be there in a couple of minutes. This will be more authentic if you don't see exactly where JJ's going to be.'

By the time JJ reached the almost vertical wall of rock, the rest of the group had already vanished up another steep track to one side of the cliff. It felt like she was completely alone with Ben, who had pulled some items from what was left of the pile of equipment the team had carried to the scene.

'One harness.' He held it up to show JJ. 'This is so your rescuer can clip you to his or her harness to make sure you're kept safe.'

JJ nodded. 'Safe is good.'

Being safe while being lifted from a rock ledge was the least of her immediate worries, however, because Ben was standing close enough to her to be causing some odd ripples of sensation in her gut.

'Three loops. One for your waist and one for each leg.' Ben gave the harness a shake. 'We don't want anything twisted.' He was crouching as he spoke. 'Put your left leg in this loop.'

It was easy enough to put all her weight on her uninjured ankle to poke her foot through the loop but JJ had no choice but to hold onto Ben's shoulder when she needed to lift the other foot. She could feel her cheeks reddening even before he began to slide the loops up her thighs.

'I can do that.'

'Take them right up. High as you can. They're elasticised so they shouldn't be either too tight or too loose.' Ben straightened up to take the ends of the waist band and thread a strap through the central buckle. He pulled it tight but then put a fingertip beneath the belt and ran it across her belly.

Dear Lord…that sensation in JJ's gut felt like a trail of small flames.

'Most important thing is to make sure that this band sits over the top of your hip bones,' Ben said. 'That way, you'll still be safe even if you get tipped upside down.'

JJ already felt as if something was being tipped upside down. She didn't dare look directly at Ben as he secured the strap by threading it through a second part of the buckle and then ducked to find her a helmet. She jammed it onto her head but then fumbled with the fastening beneath her chin.

'Here…let me.'

JJ closed her eyes as she lifted her chin. She could feel the brush of Ben's fingers on the delicate area of skin beneath her jaw bones that she'd never thought of as an erogenous zone. Until now…

She opened her eyes when she heard the buckle click shut, knowing that Ben had finished his task. The last thing she expected was that he wasn't moving away. He was staring at her and, for a moment that seemed long enough for time to have stopped, JJ was convinced he could read her thoughts.

That he knew all too well that the only thing she was thinking about was being kissed. By *him*… That, for a split second, it was possibly something she wanted more than she'd ever wanted anything else in her life.

It might have happened, too, if a two-way radio Ben had clipped to his belt hadn't crackled into life.

'We're all set, boss.' It sounded like Mike's voice. 'You planning on coming up any time soon?'

Ben didn't break his eye contact with JJ until he had the radio in his hand when it seemed like pressing the talk button flicked another switch at the same time.

'Just need to position our patient,' he radioed back. 'Do a check on everybody's harness and the Prusik loops they've used to attach their ropes. Don't let anybody go over the edge till I get up there, though.'

'Roger that.'

'Come on.' Ben jerked his head but didn't look back at JJ as he led her to where she needed to scramble up onto the ledge.

Those flames in her belly were becoming something rather more solid now, she realised as she followed Ben. Fear, perhaps?

Or was it the knowledge that an inappropriate attraction that she'd thought had been confined to the odd, hidden, middle-of-the-night type of fantasy had just exploded into something that was about to break out of that very private part of her life?

Which wouldn't be a problem, except…

Except that, in that weird moment when time had done something strange and elastic, she could have sworn that Ben had been doing more than reading her mind. He had been thinking about kissing her.

And he'd wanted it as much as she had.

# CHAPTER SIX

QUEENSTOWN.

The small, South Island town that nestled on the shores of Lake Wakatipu, in the shadows of New Zealand's dramatic Southern Alps, was widely regarded as the adventure tourism capital of the world and it was Ben Marshall's favourite place. Not simply because of the great bars and restaurants or the stunning scenery or even the lively crowd of young, mostly foreign travellers who came looking for work where an income was either a bonus or a means to an adrenaline rush. Queenstown had been the closest thing to a big town when Ben had been growing up nearby and it still felt like home. His first holiday jobs had included driving jet boats through the rapids on the Shotover River and as a coach on the ski fields in the Remarkables and the thrill of discovering adult freedom in such a vibrant atmosphere was a memory he would always treasure.

It was still the focus of his social life away from Cutler's Creek and it had been too long since he'd enjoyed this particular tapas bar on the lakefront that was also known for its great range of boutique beer. Ben took another appreciative sip of the only drink he intended having on his night off. It wasn't until he was wiping a bit of foam from the corner of his mouth with his thumb that he noticed his companion was mirroring his action—with her tongue. He looked away as he cleared his throat.

'Great idea, this, Heidi. Thanks for texting me.'

'No problem.' Coming from the French speaking part of Switzerland, Heidi's accent was as sexy as her long, platinum blonde hair, blue eyes and legs that went on for ever. 'I've been missing having Ingrid as my housemate so I thought you were probably feeling lonely like me. It seems like too long since you were in town.'

Ben was tracing drops of moisture on the outside of his beer glass with his fingertip. 'Life's been busy, I guess.'

'Really? You have a lot of exciting accidents in your little village?'

'Not often,' Ben had to admit. 'In fact, the most exciting thing in the last week or so wasn't even real. We had a practice rescue of someone stuck on a cliff with a broken ankle after an abseiling accident.'

'So you used a...what do you call them... the pretend people?'

'A mannequin? No, we used a real person only she didn't have a real broken ankle. She had sprained it not so long ago, though, so that helped her acting.'

Maybe it hadn't been purely acting. JJ's ankle was probably pretty sore after the way she'd tackled that tough track like a champion. She hadn't flinched at the prospect of being deposited on a narrow ledge, either, and putting her safety totally in the hands of a team that was still learning about difficult rescue situations—not just for being taken off that ledge but being strapped onto a stretcher and carried down the track, including that gnarly section with those big boulders in the way.

She might come across as being someone who was overly cautious and liked her environment to be organised to the nth degree but it wasn't because she lacked courage, was it? Far from it…

'So…the next time, yes?'

'Sorry?' Ben realised he hadn't heard a word of what Heidi had just said.

'The next time. I can be your patient? I can come and play with you?'

Oh, man…the invitation in those blue eyes was something any red-blooded man would probably give at least an eye tooth to be the recipient of.

'Have you eaten enough?' Heidi was sliding off the bar stool beside him. She was also sliding her hand into his. 'Shall we go for a walk?'

A walk back to her place?

Ben was perfectly happy to accept the invitation. It was, after all, the reason he'd come into town for his night off, wasn't it? Heidi was right, it had been too long and… he knew he needed this. A reminder of an important part of his life.

There was enough moonlight to be gilding the soft ripples of the lake as they walked along the beachfront, away from the busy town centre. Ben knew that Heidi's apartment was not far away but, for some strange reason, his steps were slowing. Heidi thought he needed a moment to savour the view and the tug on his hand made him stop completely.

'It's funny, isn't it?' Heidi smiled. 'I come right across the world and I love it because I find mountains that remind me of home.'

She was still holding Ben's hand as she turned to catch his gaze and it was blindingly obvious that she wanted him to kiss her but, instead of being exactly how he'd wanted this evening to progress, Ben was aware of a sinking sensation in his gut. He'd seen a look very much like this only days ago, hadn't he?

In JJ's eyes...

Dammit...this wasn't working. He still wanted to kiss JJ, which made absolutely no sense at all.

Perhaps kissing Heidi would do the trick. Desire should inevitably kick in because Heidi was exactly his type—and the total opposite of JJ Hamilton.

Except it didn't change anything. It only made it even more painfully clear that this wasn't going to work.

'I'm sorry,' he murmured, breaking what was possibly the most unsatisfying kiss he'd ever experienced. 'My head's not in the right space.'

'No worries...' Heidi shrugged. 'Next time, maybe?'

'Maybe...' Ben offered an apologetic smile as he let go of Heidi's hand.

He gave her a wave a minute later, after he'd said goodnight and was heading for where he'd parked his car.

That sinking sensation had settled into a weight inside his chest that didn't feel like it was going anywhere in a hurry. It was kind of a sad feeling.

As if he knew there wasn't going to be a next time?

'Queenstown?'

'Yes. My favourite spot in the world. I've had a holiday house there for twenty years now. And a mooring for my boat right on the waterfront. Ah...' Visiting specialist Nigel Shaw was clearly familiar with his destination as he pushed open the doors of Cutler's Creek Hospital's kitchen. 'Betty... I hope that's some of your famous vegetable soup I can smell?'

'And your favourite toasties, Dr Shaw. With cheese and mustard.'

'You know me so well, Betty.'

'Come and sit down. You, too, Dr Hamilton.'

'Thanks, Betty. Don't mind if I do.' JJ put the books she was carrying to one side as she sat down at the table. 'There's a couple of patients you saw in your cardiology clinic this morning that I should catch up with.'

'Of course. I'll do a full report for their medical records and email it through by this evening but is there someone in particular you're concerned about?'

There was a container full of cutlery in the middle of the table and another one with paper serviettes beside it. It didn't matter how many people turned up here at mealtimes because Betty always had food and a warm welcome available. In the few weeks JJ had been working here, she'd had lunch with the other doctors—Zac and Don, Bruce the policeman, various local firies and other volunteers and, of course, Ben.

JJ closed her eyes in a determined blink, as if that could stop her thoughts going in an unwanted direction. She'd put a plan into place immediately after that unfortunate moment during that training session on Twin Rocks track and she wasn't about to deviate from the programme.

'Yes. Shirley Keen. She was very anxious when I saw her last week about the palpitations she seems to still be experiencing.'

'Mmm. Her ECG was normal—apart from the changes you'd expect from someone with a BMI of thirty-five. I've ordered blood tests to rule out something like a potassium or magnesium imbalance. Hypomagnesaemia is surprisingly common.'

'Did she bring her diary in? I encouraged her to make a note of any possible triggers, like caffeine, exercise, alcohol, etcetera.'

'She said she'd forgotten.'

'To bring it or fill it in? Never mind...' JJ shook her head. 'I'll follow that up. It's not your problem.' She sniffed appreciatively as Betty put a steaming bowl of soup in front of her. 'That looks amazing.'

'Toasties are on the way. And there's plenty more soup where that came from.'

Nigel Shaw was happy to eat and discuss patients at the same time. 'We can think about doing a twenty-four-hour Holter monitor test for Shirley if you think she could cope with that. It would be helpful if you could catch any episodes of dysrhythmia on a rhythm strip and send them through to me in Dunedin. Is your ambulance service up to covering that?'

'Oh…absolutely. We've got an extremely competent paramedic in charge here.'

'Ben?' Nigel nodded his thanks to Betty as she added a platter of toasted sandwiches to the table. 'I've met him. He came up to Dunedin to do a training course we ran on thrombolytic administration in rural settings. You're lucky he's still here. I seem to remember he was talking about switching to a job with the helicopter rescue crew.'

'Oh?' The thought of Ben not being here came as a shock. Which was crazy because JJ was doing her best to convince herself that she wasn't going to let him mess with her head any longer and she had her plan in action already. Thanks to that training session, she'd realised not only how unfit she was when it came to climbing hills but how little she knew about the kinds of outdoor skills she might need in an area like Cutler's Creek so she'd embarked on an ambitious programme to improve both her fitness and knowledge.

'So…' Nigel reached for a sandwich. 'Anyone else you're worried about?'

'Thomas Sefton? I know he's got a lot

more going on than his angina. I'd really like to help him with the peripheral neuropathy that's contributing to his inability to exercise. He's worried about dependency if he goes onto an opioid based analgesic.'

Nigel smiled. 'He's ninety-three. It's really not an issue. I can have another chat with him, if you like. I'm not heading back to Dunedin until Monday. I fancied a long weekend in Queenstown. I imagine you're enjoying discovering all the local delights?'

'I'm ashamed to say I haven't explored much in the area yet. I got a bit caught up as soon as I arrived here.' JJ made a face. 'I've been bottle-raising a lamb but I've got him down to two feeds a day now so I could get away for a day.'

'Come this weekend, then. I could show you around. A vineyard tour, perhaps. Or a cruise on the lake?'

Oh, help…was this visiting cardiologist *flirting* with her? Asking her for a date, even?

'That is, if you've got free time. I haven't seen Zac around this morning, come to think of it. Or Don.'

'Don's here.' It was a relief to be able to dodge that invitation. 'He's probably in his office and hasn't realised it's lunchtime.

Zac's in Dunedin, which is a trip he's making a couple of times a week at the moment. He and Liv have a baby that arrived a bit too early.'

'I heard.'

The concern on Nigel's face made it apparent that he really cared. He was a nice man, JJ realised. And he wasn't bad looking, either. That moustache of his was impressively well trimmed. He was, in fact, just the kind of man she'd always been attracted to. Exactly her type. So why wasn't she feeling remotely interested by the attention he was giving her?

'I'm…ah…not sure exactly when Zac's due back so I can't really make plans for the weekend. Covering his gaps is the reason I'm here in the first place.'

'I understand completely. I'll console myself with my favourite pastimes of fishing and bush walks.'

Nice, safe pleasures, JJ noted. He probably loved reading interesting, non-fiction books, as well. Or watching classic movies. He should be becoming more attractive by the minute.

'I'm doing a bit of walking myself,' she found herself saying. 'With Shaun.'

Nigel blinked. 'A friend of yours?'

'The lamb I was telling you about. He follows me everywhere and is surprisingly good company for a walk. I'm trying to improve my level of fitness.'

She was walking further and faster every day, in fact, and when the challenge of flat ground and smaller hills became too easy, JJ was planning to leave Shaun at home so that she could have another go at that Twin Rocks track. How embarrassing had it been to get so out of breath in front of Ben and to need his assistance in climbing over rocks?

'Always a good thing.' Nigel nodded. Then he smiled. 'Though, in my professional opinion, I have to say you look in perfect shape already.'

Yep. This was flirting. JJ averted her gaze instantly. 'I'm learning some bushcraft, too,' she said, hoping to change the subject completely. She shifted her diary to expose the cover of the other small book she had been carrying. 'This is full of all sorts of stuff. I'm reading the chapter on how to cross rivers safely.'

Nigel reached for a serviette to wipe his mouth and fingers, turning away from JJ. 'That was delicious, as always, Betty.' Then he smiled at JJ. 'I'll head off, unless there's anyone else you want me to see or discuss? It's such a lovely afternoon, if I finish those patient reports soon, I might even get out on the lake for an hour or two.'

'Enjoy,' JJ responded, as she shook her head in response to his query. 'I've got your email address and I'll contact you if there's anything to discuss.'

'Please do.' The warmth of Nigel's smile made it crystal clear that he would welcome the contact even if it had nothing to do with a patient. Especially if it didn't…

Betty collected the plates from the table as soon as the visiting specialist had gone.

'You could do worse,' she murmured, giving JJ a wink. 'He likes you.'

'*Betty*… I don't even know if he's single.'

'He is. I believe his wife ran off with her yoga instructor a year or so ago.'

'Hmm… I wonder why?' JJ grinned. She shouldn't say anything else but she felt a sudden need to dispatch an image of how pleased her grandmother would look if she knew that JJ was dating a good looking, respected cardiologist. Someone safe. The absolute opposite of a bad boy who took risks and wasn't about to follow all the rules if he

could get away with it. And there it was...
she could see the look in Ben's eyes again.
The one that she was sure had told her that
he'd been thinking about kissing her.

Any embryonic interest in a new male ac-
quaintance evaporated instantly. 'Maybe his
wife got bored with fishing,' she muttered.

Betty headed for her sink with a snort. 'If
you're going anywhere near Doc Donaldson's
office, tell him the soup won't stay hot for
much longer.'

'No need.' It was Don Donaldson who
spoke, as he entered the kitchen. 'I caught
Nigel as he left and he told me I was late for
lunch.'

He wasn't alone.

'I'm just gatecrashing.' Ben's wide smile
was aimed at Betty. 'Your soup is as irresistible as you are, Betty.'

JJ was scrambling to her feet. Sitting
around chatting with Ben Marshall was not
part of the new plan. It was high time she got
back to work, anyway. She was a little too
quick in grabbing her books, however, and
one of them slid from her hands to land on
the floor. Ben swooped to pick it up.

'Bushcraft?' His eyes widened as he

flipped it open to where JJ's bookmark was. 'River crossing, huh?'

JJ shrugged. 'It was in the cottage. Maybe Zac left it behind. I just thought that you never know when information like that could come in handy.'

'What are you doing tomorrow?'

'What? Why?'

'Because I can teach you more about crossing a river safely than you'll ever learn by reading about it.'

'She's not doing anything,' Don put in. 'Not around here, anyway. I'm on duty.'

'You're doing a training session? On river crossings?'

'Am now.' Ben's eyebrow lifted. 'It was shaping up to be a boring afternoon given that I had nothing exciting planned and I can't stand getting bored, so how 'bout it? As you said, you never know—it could save your life one day. I'll pick you up. One p.m.?' He didn't wait for an answer because he was moving to where Betty was ladling more soup into bowls. 'I'd marry you, Betty,' he said, 'if you weren't already taken.'

She was laughing. 'Thirty years ago, lad,' she said, 'you wouldn't have stood a chance.'

It was the sound of that laughter that was

making JJ smile as she slipped out of the kitchen. Such a happy sound, it was no wonder that her day had just acquired a new glow.

'So where's everybody else?'

Good question... But the only response Ben offered was to raise his eyebrows because he didn't really have the answer. Maybe that's what he'd decided he needed to find out himself when he'd discarded the list of other potential volunteers who might appreciate some bushcraft training.

JJ's deep frown was making a furrow on her brow 'You said you were running a river crossing training course but there's nobody here except us. Are we going to wait for them?'

'I never said it was a team training session. Did I?'

'Um...no...'

Was that simply wariness in those dark eyes now? Or something more? Surprise? Pleasure, even...? The thought that JJ might like the idea they were going to spend some time alone together in the mountains created a flicker of anticipation in Ben's gut and he knew that was the key to why he'd engineered this situation even as he'd tried to talk himself out of it last night. There was something about this woman that was messing with his head. His *life*, even, given that disastrous date with Heidi the other evening. He needed to identify what that something was and deal with it.

JJ was eyeing the backpack as he eased his arms through the straps. 'You planning to stay in the high country for a week?'

He flicked a glance at the small hiker's day pack she was holding. 'You got a complete change of clothes in that? Pack liner? First aid kit? A torch, fire-lighting gear, toilet paper and a pocket knife?'

Her eyes widened, as if she hadn't realised how big a deal river crossings could be. As if she was more than a little nervous all of a sudden. But, instead of being annoying, Ben found he rather liked that idea. He could look after her. Keep her safe at the same time as teaching her something important.

'It's all good,' he added. 'That's why I've got everything we might need.'

'I've got food.' JJ's smile was hopeful. 'I made some cheese and mustard sandwiches because Betty's were so good yesterday. And I've got a Thermos of soup because I thought we might get a bit cold with wet feet. It's only tomato soup out of a can, though. My gran would be appalled.'

'My childhood favourite,' Ben told her. 'And something that *my* nan always kept in her pantry.'

Her smile faltered and he could see it was because she'd picked up on his use of the past tense.

'She died when I was fifteen.'

'Oh… I'm sorry…'

He shrugged as he turned away. 'It's a long time ago. It's not uncommon, is it, to lose your grandparents?'

'I'm lucky I've still got mine. Gran, that is. Grandad died a few years ago.'

Ben acknowledged the information with a nod but he didn't want to talk about it. He didn't talk to anyone about his nan, for that matter. Or even think about her much. He'd actually forgotten that he and JJ had something quite unusual in common, having both been raised by grandparents. Because he'd preferred to push that particular moment when he'd felt that connection with her from his mind? In the same way he'd been trying so hard to dismiss the desire to kiss this woman?

'Come on…' He knew he sounded too

abrupt but he was starting to think this whole idea might be a big mistake. 'Let's go.'

It was easy enough to steer clear of anything he didn't want to think about as they tramped upriver to find the section that Ben always used to train newbies. A typical, New Zealand braided river, Cutler's 'Creek' offered several different channels that meandered and crossed each other as they headed towards the sea. They offered varying degrees of difficulty, from easy and shallow to a stretch of white water further upstream that could challenge even experienced participants.

JJ seemed happy to listen as he explained how to choose the best place to cross a river, or even whether it was safe to cross at all.

'Look at the river from as high a place on the bank as you can find. You want to try and judge the depth and speed of the flow, whether it's over shingle or boulders and any dangers like rapids, submerged tree branches and side streams that will be adding to the water volume.' He stopped several times as they walked upstream to encourage JJ to select what she thought would be a good spot.

'There. No…that's not good, is it? Steep banks mean deep water, don't they? And they can make it impossible to get out on the other side. And what happens if you get swept off your feet further up from banks like that?'

'I'm not intending to let you get swept off your feet,' Ben told her. 'This is River Crossing for Beginners and I'll be hanging onto you.' He could start teaching her the techniques to keep herself safe, floating with the current, when they got to a more difficult crossing.

There were two variations of the mutual support method that Ben taught. They both involved putting an arm around each other's backs and getting a good grip on either a pack strap or clothing. Even teaching JJ to take small, shuffling steps, not to lift her feet too high in the water and to watch the far bank as much as possible so as not to get disoriented by the flow of the river wasn't enough to distract him from the awareness that his hands were touching her body.

And maybe that was why he wasn't holding quite tightly enough when JJ slipped on a small boulder when they were in the middle of their second crossing—this time in knee-level water with a faster current. He kept his promise to hang onto her but, try as he might, he couldn't keep them both upright and the current was strong enough to sweep them downstream just far enough for them both to be soaked from head to foot by the time he found his footing again and managed to pull JJ onto the safety of a shingle island between two channels.

Just far enough for JJ to have swallowed a bit of water that was making her cough, for her to have become cold enough to be shivering badly already and to have scared her so much she looked a great deal younger than she actually was.

So vulnerable that Ben could feel something melting inside his chest. A liquid kind of feeling that matched the external river water that was streaming from his clothes and hair, except that the internal sensation was a lot more powerful and it was spreading throughout his entire body.

Good grief, it even seemed to be reaching his eyes.

'It's okay,' he heard himself saying aloud as he pulled JJ into his arms. 'It's okay… you're safe now… I've got you…'

# CHAPTER SEVEN

HOW TERRIFYING HAD that been?

The fear hadn't kicked in in that first moment when she'd felt her foot lose contact with the boulder beneath it because that had happened too fast. The shock of being plunged into water that felt like barely melted ice was so great that JJ didn't have the brain space to feel frightened then, either. It was when she felt the power in that current tipping her so that she couldn't get her face out of the water, the brush of a large rock beneath her that she'd probably just missed hitting her head on and she realised how easy it could be to drown that fear not only kicked in but instantly ramped up to terror.

Not that the intensity of that terror had lasted for more than a heartbeat. Or maybe two. Because she'd known that Ben still had a grip on her. She was trusting him with her life but she had no choice and, at some level, she knew that trust wasn't misplaced. And she'd been right. Here she was, out of the water. Safe. Shaking like a leaf, of course, but she was safe. Ben was holding her in his arms and, to be honest, JJ had never felt so safe in her life. How crazy was that?

Crazy enough to make her laugh, anyway, as she pulled back to look up at Ben.

'River C-Crossing for Beginners, huh?' Her teeth were chattering hard enough to make her stutter. 'I'd h-hate to do one of y-your advanced classes.'

'You're the first person I've dropped in a river,' Ben told her. 'Sorry about that.'

'I wasn't h-holding on tightly enough,' JJ confessed. 'And I was l-looking d-down...'

'And you're freezing. Come on. Hopefully the extra clothing in my pack will have stayed dry enough.'

The channels they needed to negotiate to get back to the riverbank where they'd started this training session got progressively easier and Ben was certainly keeping a tight grip on JJ but she was so cold ten minutes later that her fingers refused to co-operate by holding onto the strap of Ben's backpack.

Even her legs didn't seem to want to hold her up.

'How f-far?' she asked. 'To the car?'

'We're not going to the car,' Ben responded. 'Not yet. With this wind picking up, you'll be hypothermic in no time. There's a hut a lot closer. Just basic but we can get a fire going and some dry clothes on.' He grinned at JJ. 'Think of it as your survival training session.'

The hut was small. Just a single room with a couple of old, wooden chairs, a tiny table and a pot-bellied stove but it was a huge relief to be out of the wind.

'Get those clothes off,' Ben ordered, as he opened his pack. 'Yes…that dunk wasn't enough to get right into the sealed bags in here. I've got a pair of trackpants and a sweatshirt that you can put on. There's a foil sheet in here if they're not enough.'

'What about you?'

'There's an extra pair of trackpants but I'll be fine for the moment while I get this fire going. I've got merino thermals on.' He handed her the bag. 'Take everything wet off,' he instructed. 'It won't take long to get your undies dry and, by the time we've got warm and had something to eat, everything

else will be at least wearable for the trek back
to the car.'

But JJ barely heard the last of his words.
He wanted her to take her *underwear* off?
She should be horrified at the thought. So
why was there suddenly a heat in parts of her
body that couldn't possibly be explained by
simply having shelter from the wind? This
didn't make sense. Any more than her reaction had, when she'd discovered that there
weren't going to be any other people joining them on this training session. She should
have been annoyed by that. Feeling manipu-
lated, perhaps. Instead, she'd been secretly
pleased because it made her feel...special?

Ben let his breath out in an amused huff
at her expression. 'Don't worry, I won't be
looking.' He peeled his anorak off, leaving
it to hang and drip from a large hook on the
wall. 'I've got enough to do making a fire,
here. If you hurry up, I can show you how
to shave kindling off pieces of wood that are
too big—like those logs in the corner, there.'

He was crouched in front of the stove by
the time he finished speaking, a pocket knife
in one hand and a piece of wood in the other.
He had his back to JJ so he couldn't possibly
see what she was doing and she turned her

own back on him as she began to peel sodden clothing away from her body but this still felt incredibly…wrong, somehow. Naughty, even? Certainly something that rule-following people shouldn't be doing.

Something a *boring* person would never dream of doing, that's for sure, but JJ was in the middle of an adventure, here, wasn't she? She'd just been washed down a river, for heaven's sake. Saved from drowning by the kind of hero any woman would dream of being rescued by—someone who was even giving up his own, spare clothing so that she could be warm and dry.

No wonder she was feeling a very different appreciation of life right now. Or that rules she had lived by her entire life seemed suddenly irrelevant.

She'd known from when she was old enough to start asking questions that it had been her mother's fault that her grandparents had lost their beloved only son. She'd been driving the van that day. Touring around Europe had been her idea—something their sensible boy would never have considered doing if he hadn't fallen in love with someone as wild as JJ's mother. It didn't mean that JJ had been any less loved, of course. It just meant that they'd made sure she understood what she needed to do to stay safe, for her own sake and for the people who loved her.

She'd always known that she had to fight any inclination to be anything like her mother.

JJ had done that literally by accident today. But, instead of being consumed by guilt, she was feeling more alive than she ever had and there was no way she was going to fight this kind of exhilaration. For perhaps the first time ever, she could understand why her mother had chosen to live her life like that. Maybe it was also no wonder that JJ had to bite back a smile as her cold fingers fumbled with the catch on her bra strap.

He couldn't see what JJ was doing.

But he *knew* what she was doing and he could imagine that wet clothing being peeled from her skin to leave it exposed. He could even imagine the goose bumps that would give it a texture that could only be smoothed by warmth—like the fire he was building, or the warmth from the touch of another person, perhaps?

Oh...man... Even being thoroughly chilled himself and making sure he was distracted by a physical activity that he needed to focus on if he didn't want to slice a good part of this thumb off wasn't stopping the heat of his body's reaction to what was going on behind him.

This was what the problem was with JJ Hamilton, wasn't it?

Despite the fact that she was so unlike any other woman he'd ever been attracted to before—or perhaps *because* of that—this attraction was off the scale. It was far more than attraction. More than desire, even. This was lust, pure and simple but that was okay. He could control it. Hide it, in fact, given that he was a very long way from being some inexperienced teenager.

Ben gave JJ plenty of time to get out of her clothes and into the dry ones. He had the fire crackling by then and had taken off his own outer shirt to leave just the short-sleeved, close-fitting merino thermal against his skin. He moved to shift the wooden chairs close to the stove to use as a clothes rack to speed up the drying process and, even then, he avoided looking directly at JJ but he caught what was happening from the corner of his eye. He saw the most perfect, naked butt disappearing beneath the trackpants she was pulling up and he had to close his eyes as he let his breath out very, very slowly. He needed to clear his throat, too, before he could hope that his voice would sound normal.

'We'll hang all the wet stuff over these chairs by the fire.'

'Okay.' JJ wasn't about to notice anything odd in his expression. She was looking down at the old, soft sweatshirt of his. 'I really like this. Red is my favourite colour.'

'Keep it,' Ben told her. 'It suits you.'

JJ handed back the bag he'd used for the spare clothing. 'Here…you can get this other pair of dry pants on now.'

'I'll help you wring as much water as we can from your clothes first.'

JJ's hair was still soaked and the end of her long braid was making a damp patch on the front of the red sweatshirt. Ben tried very hard not to look at it. Or think about what was underneath that damp patch. JJ didn't seem bothered. She worked briskly, wringing out the smaller items of clothing and then draping them over the rungs on the back of her chairs.

Good grief…who knew that someone that came across as being so uptight would wear underwear that was so lacy it had to be pretty much see-through?

Ben finally stripped off his wet trousers, leaving his merino long johns on as he reached for the other pair of dry trackpants that JJ had left on the table. She didn't even look in his direction. She was busy pulling something from her small pack.

'Oh…no…'

'What?' She had something in her hand. Something that was dripping through her fingers and Ben found himself grinning broadly. 'Yeah…sandwiches don't usually like getting wet.'

Her face lit up as she returned his smile and for a long, long moment they held eye contact that made the room seem an awful lot smaller than it had a minute or two ago.

It was JJ who finally broke that gaze as her smile faded.

'Yuk…' she murmured, dropping the bulk of what she was holding back into the wrapping. 'At least the soup should be okay.'

Her hand was still covered in a sticky mess. Without thinking, Ben reached out to wipe it clean with the soft fabric in his hands.

Startled, she looked up at him again and, this time, he could actually feel the flash of something igniting. Maybe it was because they were skin to skin where he was holding her hand. Or maybe it was because he could see her eyes darken even more than they were naturally—as if her pupils were dilating. Or…maybe this had just been waiting to happen ever since he'd first laid eyes on this woman.

Whatever caused the spark, it wasn't going to fizzle out any time soon. It had, in fact, found some real fuel—like that match Ben had been holding against wood shavings in what suddenly felt like a very long time ago. He knew that JJ wasn't about to break this gaze. He could feel a solid wave of exactly the same level of desire that was currently taking over every cell in his own body.

Ben wasn't going to break the gaze, either. He held it as he dropped the fabric he was holding and lifted his hand to touch her face. With one finger, he traced the outline of her temple and cheekbone and then down the side of her nose. He watched as JJ's eyes drifted shut as his finger touched the corner of her mouth and then tracked along her lower lip, so gently he could feel only the tingle of that incredibly soft skin. When her lips parted and he felt the tip of her tongue touch his finger, Ben knew he was completely lost.

So, apparently, was JJ, judging by the way she came up on her tiptoes as he cupped the back of her head and tilted back to offer her mouth to his. And this was no gentle, exploratory first kiss. He'd been right to think that this had been waiting to happen. There was a sense that an unbearable tension was being finally released, here. That this was something they'd both wanted for too long and it couldn't happen fast enough. Dear Lord, he already had his hands beneath the oversized sweatshirt JJ was wearing. Was it that damp patch that was making her nipple as hard as a pebble from the creek, or was it the touch of his hand that was arousing her so much? And, if it was, he could only dream of how she might react to the slippery warmth of his tongue.

This was happening too fast but it felt like neither of them wanted it to slow down. Or stop it going a whole lot further except…this was breaking a rule that Ben had never broken in his adult life. How could he, when his own mother had told him that her unplanned pregnancy had ruined her life?

'We can't do this…' It was the hardest

thing he'd ever done, pulling back from that kiss. That touch. But it had to be done. 'It's not safe…'

Of course it wasn't safe.

This was the most reckless thing JJ had ever done in her life. She was about to have sex with a real-life bad boy. The kind of man she'd wouldn't have gone near in a million years in her previous life because she'd known better than to do something wild and be accused of 'being just like her mother'. She might very well never do it again so she knew that if she didn't do it now, she would lose a once-in-a-lifetime opportunity to see whether real life was anything like the kind of fantasies she'd been playing with.

And it wasn't *un*safe. Not in the way Ben was worried about, anyway.

'I'm on the Pill,' she told him.

She could feel his breath on her face as he closed his eyes, leaning in to touch her nose with his. She could feel his hands on her waist, his fingers closing in to shape the hollows just above her hip bones.

'You want this?' His voice was so deep it was like the crunch of gravel beneath feet. 'As much as I do…?'

The shaft of sensation his fingers were creating was moving diagonally from her hips, nosediving to pool in the place she most needed him to touch her.

'Yes…' JJ's voice was as raw as Ben's. She couldn't bear it if he stopped. He mustn't stop. *'Please…'*

They didn't make it to the dusty floorboards of that hut. JJ felt the rough wood of the wall behind her back by the time the second most astonishing kiss of her life had ended. Somehow, they shifted their clothing enough to get their skin touching exactly where it was needed and JJ was oblivious to the danger of splinters in her back as Ben finally cupped her buttocks and lifted her feet from the floor to perfect their alignment. She wrapped her arms around his neck and her legs around his waist—a move she'd only ever read about before but it felt astonishingly natural. Easy.

And safe…as safe as she had been in Ben's arms when he'd pulled her from the river. Only this time she could let go and float with the current of a building pleasure like nothing she'd ever known existed.

The cry of ecstasy that came from her throat a short time later was also like no

sound she'd ever heard herself make. But, then, she'd never experienced anything like this before, had she? She'd just been taken by a bad boy. In a way that made it feel like she'd just lost her virginity all over again.

Nothing was ever going to be the same.

'Wow...' As post-coital conversation, this wasn't impressive but Ben was still having trouble finding any words in an almost awkward space of time when they had finally recovered enough to pull themselves apart. He had to lean in to kiss JJ again, though. Softly, this time, because passion that exploded that ferociously couldn't possibly happen again.

Or maybe it could... The touch—and taste—of JJ's lips felt familiar now but it was just as exciting. Ben closed his eyes.

'What just happened there?' he murmured.

'I'm not sure.' JJ's voice was no more than a whisper but he could hear the smile in it. 'But...it was...um...really good.'

Ben groaned. 'I know...and it shouldn't have been.'

'Why not?' There was a wary note in her voice now. 'Because it was...boring?'

His breath came out in an incredulous huff. 'Are you *kidding* me? Boring is the last word on earth I'd use to describe what we just did.'

'But you thought it shouldn't have been good?'

'Yeah…' He wasn't about to admit that he'd hadn't believed a real sexual encounter with JJ would be anything like as good as any fantasy he might or might not have considered. 'Because…no offence, JJ, but you're so not my type.'

This time there was a hint of laughter in her voice. 'And you couldn't be further from my type. You're right, it shouldn't have worked at all.'

Ben opened his eyes to catch her gaze. 'But it did, didn't it?' He kissed her again. 'Okay…if I'm honest, I've been wanting to do this for a long time.'

'Mmm…'

That sound was pretty much an admission of the same thing, wasn't it?

'So…' Ben knew they both needed to move closer to the fire and start getting properly warm but JJ wasn't shivering any more and he could feel the warmth of her skin against his own. 'Did we get it out of our systems, do you think? Enough to go back to our usual "types"?'

There was a flicker in JJ's eyes that could have been amusement. Or possible a desire to do it all over again?

'I'm not sure,' she said. 'What do you think?'

Ben could feel his mouth curling on one side. 'I'm not sure, either. But I do think we should pick somewhere more comfortable for next time.'

Oh, yeah…that was definitely desire he could see in her eyes. But she broke her gaze, as if she didn't want him to see how much she wanted a 'next time'.

'It's not as though it's going to last,' she said, slipping away and pulling that sweatshirt down to cover herself properly. 'I'm only here until things settle down for Zac and he's back on deck full time but, even if I was here for ever, it wouldn't last, would it? Not when we're so completely incompatible.'

'True. I'm not even going to be around that much longer. I've been thinking of moving on for a long time now. I'm determined to get some helicopter rescue training in at some point in my career.'

Ben knew that the extraordinary physical pleasure they'd just discovered with each other was purely down to lust and would burn itself out in no time but it was a relief to hear that JJ recognised that, as well. He'd been curious about an unexpected attraction and, while it had been infinitely better than he might have imagined, of course it wasn't going to last.

It never did. Even with the women who were a hundred percent his 'type'.

But who wouldn't want to enjoy it for as long as it *did* last?

How weird was this?

JJ was acting as though nothing momentous had just happened. Like she had casual sex with bad boys all the time. She was even getting that Thermos of very ordinary tomato soup out of her pack like they were about to have a picnic or something but maybe she just needed to do something with her hands.

Other than touching Ben Marshall.

Maybe she needed a distraction from the words that were echoing in her head but that she could feel deep down in her belly.

Next time…

It wasn't as though she was behaving totally irresponsibly here. She was just doing something she'd never considered doing before so maybe it was simply a delayed teenage rebellion. Something everybody needed to do before they really knew what they wanted from their life?

Finding that out had been the reason she'd come here in the first place, wasn't it?

And maybe this was it, in a nutshell?

Passion.

Something she'd never dared to play around with. A glimpse into what life could be like if she wasn't so bound by the rules and expectations she clung to. A glimpse into the kind of person her mother had apparently been and…maybe that *wasn't* as bad as she'd grown up believing? Being adventurous, spontaneous, passionate wasn't necessarily a recipe for the destruction of lives, was it? She'd seen other people not only get away with it but experience a joy in life she was unfamiliar with. It wasn't as if she'd want to spend her future with someone like Ben, of course, because they both knew that could never work.

But, oh, boy…it could be fun for a while.

JJ had worked so hard and diligently all her life. Followed every rule and made sure that nobody thought she was anything like as irresponsible as the mother she knew only from faded photographs. She deserved a bit of fun, didn't she? She and Ben were both adults and it wasn't as if anyone was going to get hurt.

She turned her head to smile at Ben, who was rearranging their wet clothing over the chairs by the stove.

'Soup? It's still nice and hot and I reckon it's probably just as good as your nan used to make.'

The smile she was getting in return as Ben walked towards her felt like it was reaching right inside her body. Lighting it up.

Oh, yeah…who wouldn't want to make the most of this kind of fun while it lasted? And if 'next time' was even half as good as the first time, how could she possibly resist?

She couldn't, of course.

For the simple reason that she didn't want to.

## CHAPTER EIGHT

FOR SOMETHING THAT should never have worked in the first place, it was quite remarkable how it could not only continue to work but to get better.

Every single time.

Right from that first day when they'd only stayed in the hut long enough to have a hot drink and get properly warm because an hour's hike back to Ben's vehicle wasn't a big problem, even wearing still-damp clothes. There was a long, hot shower waiting for them back at JJ's cottage, after all, not to mention a chance to deal with the astonishing level of desire that had apparently already rebuilt—on both sides. That 'next time' wasn't half as good as the first time.

It had been twice as good.

The final discovery that day had been that even the comfort of a soft mattress and warm duvet—the only kind of environment JJ had considered appropriate for this kind of activity in her previous life—didn't make the sex any less exciting. If anything, it revealed that her partners in the past had been either sadly lacking in expertise or she simply hadn't been attracted enough to flick a switch she'd never known existed. A switch that seemed to open a connection that encouraged her to be more adventurous than she could have believed and enabled her to not only receive unimaginable pleasure but to give it, as well.

JJ had expected the novelty to wear off, of course. Or for Ben to get bored and move on—probably to another one of those gorgeous blonde adrenaline junkie visitors to this part of the world—but it didn't happen. Maybe that was because Ben crammed so much into his life he was almost always busy and that meant he could only find a night or two a week to visit JJ at her cottage and he never stayed the whole night, not just because they wanted to keep their connection as private as possible but because Ben always seemed to have an early start the next day for a shift or a meeting or a fitness session.

A week sped past and then another and

another. Until neither of them were counting. Until Shaun had become a small sheep rather than a lamb. He didn't need bottle-feeding any longer and was earning his treats of sheep nuts by wearing a collar and chain and being a lawnmower around the cottage.

Locals were getting used to seeing him trotting behind JJ when she went for a run along the road and they weren't surprised when Ben began to be seen regularly in her company. It was common knowledge that he was helping her with her fitness levels, after all, but Cutler's Creek's ambulance station manager was working hard to get everybody who was involved in the emergency services around here up to speed in both fitness and bushcraft skills. He had even inspired others to jump in and help.

Everyone had splinter skills, it seemed. Bruce was an expert in creating shelters by using whatever materials might be at hand and the group that his training day attracted included people from as far away as Queenstown and the West Coast—a surprising number of whom were already becoming familiar faces to JJ. When Bruce produced a map of the huts that were available on public land and she and Ben exchanged a very private glance, she felt even more a part of this group.

It turned out to be one of the best days ever, learning how to use fly sheets or natural features like big rocks and overhangs and gather dead tussock grass, fern fronds or moss to create a surprisingly comfortable and warm mattress. You could even pull some of the dry material over your head, apparently, to trap air and retain body warmth.

Bruce also had an old school mate who'd worked in the Meteorological Service before retiring back to Central Otago and he gave a fascinating lecture in the town's school hall about how to read weather maps or the clouds and spot an approaching front that could develop into a potentially dangerous storm. Wispy clouds that were called 'mares' tails' were a sign of high-level winds and were often the first sign of bad weather. Fluffy, cumulus clouds could develop ominously dark bases and go on to signal the imminent arrival of a low-pressure system that could bring high winds, heavy rain and even snow at almost any time of the year.

JJ herself had given a talk about first aid kits—what to put in them and how to use the contents—that had also attracted interest from all over the area and, on that occasion, she not only felt a part of the group but that she was making a real contribution to this community.

Each new training session, in addition to every new or returning patient treated at the hospital, made local faces more familiar and personalities better known. JJ could look back at her arrival here and be amused by how she'd felt like a fish out of water and that she'd worried about how isolated and potentially lonely a sparsely populated area could be for a city girl like herself. She'd been far lonelier in that crowded apartment building in Wellington. Cutler's Creek was beginning to feel very much like a real home and creating a sensation of belonging that was something very new for JJ.

It felt like she was putting down tendrils of roots that could ground her for ever if they were allowed to keep growing. She was coming to love being near the mountains and the feeling of freedom that came from the open farmland. She liked these people and she admired their spirit of adventure, ingenuity and their generosity in spending so much time and effort on things that were designed to let them help others who might get into trouble in the great outdoors.

Not that she could stay *here* for ever, given that Don Donaldson wasn't showing any signs of wanting to retire yet, but maybe she could find something similar. New Zealand was a big enough country to need lots of doctors in rural areas. She might need to make the move before those roots got any deeper, mind you, because it was only going to get harder to pull them out.

'What's that face all about?' Ben was in the kitchen of Cutler's Creek Hospital as JJ walked in for a cup of coffee mid-afternoon, after the outpatient maternity clinic that she'd and midwife Debbie had been running had finished.

'Just thinking.' But JJ's heart had lifted as soon as she'd seen him and she could feel her frown evaporating.

'Hard work, was it?'

Oh…that cheeky grin. It was something else she was going to miss about this place, that was for sure.

'I'm just wondering if I'll be able to take Shaun with me when I leave Cutler's Creek, that's all.'

Betty dropped the pan she was scrubbing

in the sink with a clatter. 'You're not planning on leaving us, are you?'

'I was only ever here on a locum basis, Betty.' JJ poured herself a cup of coffee and then sat down at the table. There was a basket, lined with a tea towel, full of freshly made date scones and a big pat of butter on a plate beside them. 'Doc Donaldson tells me that the mighty Hugo is doing so well he's going to come home in the next week or so and that means that Zac will be back onboard full time very soon.' JJ reached for a scone and tried to keep her tone cheerful. 'I might have to start looking for a new job sooner rather than later.'

'Don't think Shaun would be very impressed with living in your apartment in Wellington,' Ben said.

'I might not be going back to Wellington.'

'Where might you go?' The quirk of Ben's eyebrow was a sure sign he was interested in her plans.

What would his expression reveal, JJ wondered, if she told him she might like to find another rural position, maybe even close to Cutler's Creek? That it might be possible for them to continue seeing each other every so often? As friends, of course.

Really close friends.

The kind that could pick up where they'd left off—even when it included the kind of intimacy that JJ would never have considered enjoying on a casual basis. She didn't want to consider it now, actually, but it would be better than knowing it was gone for ever, wouldn't it?

'The world is my oyster.' JJ tried to sound nonchalant. 'Coming here has taught me I can start a completely new life and…do anything I want, really…' She grinned at Ben as she caught his gaze. 'Maybe I don't want that to stop.'

She held his gaze for a heartbeat longer. Hopefully just long enough for him to get the message that their unexpected friendship was one of the things she didn't want to stop.

'Hmph.' Betty wasn't sounding impressed. 'Don't hold with things changing so fast,' she muttered. 'Not when we've just got used to the way they are.'

'Everything changes, Betty.' The scone Ben was pulling apart was still steaming. 'Except how good your cooking is. You never know, I might head off myself one of these days.' Judging by the subtle wink he gave JJ, he was quite aware of the way Betty was glaring at his back. 'I reckon JJ's right about doing what you want to do and maybe it's about time I did something about what *I've* always wanted to do and got myself a job on one of those choppers. Hey...' He turned to offer the older woman one of his most charming smiles. 'I'd still see you, Betty. Look how often the helicopter gets called in here. I could...you know...send you a text so that you could have some soup and toasties ready...'

Betty looked as though she was about to tell him that he wouldn't necessarily be welcome in her kitchen simply for free food but she didn't get the chance to say anything because Ben's pager sounded and he immediately reached for his phone.

'What's happening?'

JJ could hear the town's civil defence warning sounding as Ben was listening to the information. She could imagine Mike and Chris and Bruce, amongst others, dropping whatever they were doing right now to rush to their stations. Within minutes Bruce would be on the road in his police car, Mike would have the fire truck ready to go as soon as any volunteers arrived and Chris would be outside the ambulance station ready to jump in as Ben went past. Others would be waiting for news, as well. JJ could see Betty glancing towards the pantry, as if she was wondering what stocks were like in case something big was happening and she might need to feed some hungry crews.

'Roger that,' Ben said, ending the call as he got to his feet. 'I'm on my way.'

'What is it?' JJ asked.

'Camper van's gone over the edge in the gorge. It's wedged in rocks halfway down the cliff by Goat's Corner. No indication of how many passengers or what condition they're in.' Ben was already halfway out the door but JJ was right behind him.

'I'll come with you. Just let me grab the pack and my overalls.'

He stopped so abruptly that JJ would have banged into him if he hadn't put his hands out to catch her arms.

'No.' He was shaking his head. 'I don't want you to come this time.'

JJ's jaw dropped. She'd been out with him often enough in the last few weeks that it was becoming a normal part of her work routine. Possibly her favourite part.

Ben must have seen her bewilderment at his decision. That she was hurt, even? She knew he was poised to move fast but he wasn't going to leave her looking like that.

'It's a camper van,' he said softly. 'Down a cliff. There could be fatalities and...' His eyes were as dark as she'd ever seen them. '...and that's the way your parents died, isn't it?'

He'd remembered something she'd told him what seemed a long time ago now. A muttered comment that had been part of her trying to get past the embarrassment of him finding out her real first name. She'd said that she didn't remember anything about the accident but he still didn't want her to see something similar. Did he think it might spark some kind of flashback that could be emotionally traumatic? Was he trying to protect her?

Because he cared...?

It only took a split second for JJ's world to change. To shift on its axis as much as it had that first time Ben had kissed her. More, in fact. Because, this time, her reaction wasn't simply physical. The idea that this man cared enough to try and protect her went so deep it felt like her soul had just captured that emotion and recognised it as a missing piece.

It only took that tiny fraction of time for

JJ to understand just how much *she* cared about Ben.

A blip of time so fast that Ben only had time to turn away from her while she realised that she might actually be falling in love with him.

So fast that it was easy to pretend it had never happened. Okay, so she might have to think about it later but not right now. There was something far more urgent happening. Something that many people in this community were a part of. And JJ was part of this community now and wanted to remain a part of it for as long as possible.

'It's really not a problem,' she called, picking up speed. She caught up with Ben as he entered the hospital foyer. 'I can do this,' she told him. 'I want to come. Please…?'

It was a good thing that JJ was in the front passenger seat of the ambulance because Chris was nowhere to be seen in front of the station as Ben drove past, despite him being on call as a volunteer responder today. Maybe he was out of cell phone range somewhere on the back of the family farm or he'd had a problem with his car. Ben could call in another volunteer but he'd much rather have

JJ with him, despite the likelihood that this callout would prove to be far more challenging than anything she'd had to face so far when she'd been out on the road with him. He could only hope that her own confidence in being able to deal with it—emotionally, as well as professionally—was not misplaced.

He hit the switch to activate his beacons and siren as he put his foot down to get through the township and onto the open road that led to the gorge. There was no additional information on what they were heading for yet. Bruce was almost on scene, had set up a road block at this end of the gorge and would be able to position himself to stop any traffic coming in the opposite direction but, even with the road clear, nobody would be able to get near the camper van until Mike had the fire truck in position to provide any necessary stabilisation of the crashed vehicle. A rescue helicopter crew from Dunedin was on its way because winching someone down the sides of the steep gorge might be the only way to reach any victims.

Even at the speeds Ben was pushing his ambulance, it was going to take some time to get to Goat's Corner, which was a notorious bend about halfway into the dramatic gorge with the river far below the level of the road. Between the radio messages updating him on the activity of everybody being scrambled to deal with this emergency and the automatic thought processes of running through any likely protocols for dealing with critically injured patients, Ben was aware of snatches of thoughts about the woman on the passenger seat beside him.

Of just how wrong his first impressions of JJ Hamilton had been.

That impression of her total neatness in her designer jeans and pricey boots was only a faded memory now. Kind of amusing, when a sideways glance showed her wearing a pair of steel-capped boots and that ugly, orange, long-sleeved pair of overalls that were thick enough to protect skin from superficial injuries.

Had he really pegged her as unbearably prim and proper as well?

Ha! Even Ben's total focus on the road in front of him and the upcoming corners leading into the gorge couldn't stop the flash of remembering that what he'd experienced in that high country hut totally blew that impression out of the water.

And as for sticking religiously to protocols

and rules, she wasn't saying anything about
the way he was pushing the ambulance to
the edge of safety as the wheels clung to the
road around the tight curves of this narrow
road. He was breaking all the normal road
rules, the way he was crossing the centre line
at times. How far he was breaking the speed
limit. A glance at JJ's face, in fact, revealed a
gleam in her eyes that he recognised all too
easily and any doubts about her being on this
callout evaporated.

He knew that she didn't lack courage.
She'd taught him that when she'd been up
for anything he'd thrown her way that day
she'd pushed herself up Twin Rocks track
and agreed to be their patient for cliff rescue training. There was more than bravery in
her eyes right now, however. Ben could see
what he knew was a potent mix of professional concern about what they might have
to treat and the adrenaline rush of potentially
putting one's own life in jeopardy to save the
lives of others. A balancing act of tempering
risk factors with a determination to succeed.

He wouldn't have believed this version of
JJ Hamilton had even existed that first day
he'd met her. And it occurred to Ben that
maybe she wouldn't have believed it either

but that was the last, fleeting thought he had on the subject because as he rounded another corner he could see the flashing lights of Bruce's police car blocking any oncoming traffic.

They were on scene.

# CHAPTER NINE

JJ HAD ASSURED Ben that this callout would not be a problem but, as she stood on the roadside, looking down an almost sheer cliff to where the camper van was lying on the driver's side, wedged onto a ledge between the cliff and a huge, protruding lump of rock, she had a moment of serious doubt that she'd been telling the truth.

This was…shocking.

At first glance, it looked very unlikely that anybody had survived this crash but who knew? This wasn't an old VW Kombi, it was a modern, square white box and it probably had airbags and other safety features everywhere. Was it a young couple in there who had just had their love of life and dreams of adventure come to a crashing halt? Did they have a baby in a car seat, perhaps?

And how were they even going to find

out? How could they get down to that crumpled vehicle and, if they could, how on earth could you treat a badly injured patient in a space like that? JJ was experienced enough and had confidence in her own skills to deal with any level of trauma but maybe that only applied when she was in her nice, safe environment of an emergency department with medics and equipment and all manner of other resources that she could summon. Where were the protocols for dealing with something like this?

What rules needed to be followed in a situation that looked so dangerous that the only direction that might have been sensible would be to stay as far away as possible?

Ben was the one who really wasn't bothered, here. He was pulling big coils of rope and other climbing gear from a compartment on the side of the fire truck and having a conversation with Mike between the directions he was shouting for his team. There were steel cables being rolled out from the back of the fire truck. Someone was laying out the pneumatic cutting gear on a tarpaulin and another crew member was lowering a long ladder over the edge of the cliff. Bruce knew exactly what he was doing as well and there was a long line of traffic already held up behind where his police car was parked sideways, its beacons flashing, to block both sides of the road.

It was a relief when Ben came towards JJ. 'You okay?'

JJ nodded. She was better than she had been a moment ago, at least, when she'd been standing here alone. Just having Ben by her side was enough to make her feel considerably braver.

'Put this harness on. And a hard hat.'

'We're going to abseil down?' JJ tried to stamp on her fear but her training sessions hadn't yet got as far as learning the skills she would need to be able to do that safely.

'No. Mike's got a ladder in place to cover the first twenty metres or so. Someone's going down to get steel cables hooked onto the vehicle to stabilise it and there'll be other ropes to use. The harness is so you can have a line attached for safety at any time. It might also be useful if we need to get winched out for any reason when the chopper gets here.'

Safety... That one word stood out enough for JJ to find the courage she needed.

Ben was helping her into the harness. 'You could also wait up here until we can extract any patients but it could take a while. We don't know yet whether we'll need to get cutting gear down the hill to get them out.' He caught her gaze and held it. 'It's your choice, JJ.'

'I came here to help. Not much point in standing back and just watching, is there?'

'That's my girl…'

There was a gleam in Ben's eyes that could be interpreted as pride. Definitely approval, anyway, and his words gave JJ more than courage. There was determination there as well now. She might not know what she should be doing but she could trust that Ben did. And she wasn't about to let him down. More than anything, she wanted to be the person Ben thought she was. Someone he had reason to be proud of. *His* girl…?

There was limited room on the rocks around the van so they had to wait until some of the fire service crew came back up, having secured the ladder, cables and ropes.

'Vehicle's stable. It's well caught in the rocks but we've got cables on, as well. You're good to go.'

'Occupants?'

'Two people. Older. The driver's not responsive. There's a woman in the passenger seat and she doesn't seem too bad. Terrified, though. We've left Jack talking to her until you guys get down. Her name's Glenys.'

'Access?'

'Front door's jammed but the side door is partially open. We'll get some gear sorted and should be able to get access that way.'

Ben nodded. 'I'll go first,' he told JJ. 'And have the pack lowered at the same time.' One corner of his mouth lifted. 'That way I'll be at the bottom and ready to catch you if you're not good with ladders or ropes.'

The worst part for JJ was having to push past the fear of lowering herself over the edge of the cliff and getting onto the ladder in the first place. This had to be the most dangerous thing she'd ever done but nothing was going to stop her. Because Ben was waiting for her at the bottom? Thank goodness she'd been working on her fitness level for weeks now. She needed the strength she had gained in her muscles, especially when it came to hanging onto ropes to get over sharp edges of rock above the ledge.

Ben had swapped places with Jack the firie as JJ climbed more rock to get high enough to see into the passenger side of the camper van. A white-haired woman had a laceration in the middle of a lump on her forehead and several trickles of blood down her face.

'Hello…' Ben leaned closer to the broken window. 'You're Glenys, aren't you? I'm Ben. I'm a paramedic. And this is my partner JJ, who's a doctor.'

His partner. JJ liked the sound of that. She managed to edge a little closer.

'We're going to look after you until we can get you out. Can you remember what happened?'

'It was all so fast… I think Derek fainted. I tried to hold the steering wheel but he fell towards me and pushed me away…'

'Were you knocked out?'

'I… No, I don't think so…'

'Headache?'

'A bit…'

'Are you feeling sick or dizzy at all?'

'I'm…just really scared…'

JJ's heart went out to the woman who had to be close to her own grandmother's age, yet she was adventurous enough to have been on the road for a camping trip. She listened as Ben sped through an initial survey to try and find out how badly injured Glenys was.

She was talking well, which meant her airway was clear and her breathing adequate.

She also seemed alert enough to suggest that the bump on her head wasn't severe enough to have caused a brain injury. She might have injured her neck, however. Elderly patients could have significant C-spine trauma and show few or no neurological symptoms.

'Please...' Glenys was pleading with Ben. 'Don't worry about me. Can't you check on Derek first? He's...not moving and...' Her face crumpled in distress. 'I think he might be...it might be...too late...'

If her husband had collapsed at the wheel it was very likely that a medical event, such as a heart attack or a stroke, had been responsible for this crash. It took no more than a glance at the slumped figure on the other side of the van to see unmistakeable signs, like the colour of Derek's skin and the total absence of any visible respiratory effort or other movement, that Glenys's fears were correct.

Even if Derek had initially survived the crash, the position he was in now, with his chin on his chest, would have occluded his airway completely when he'd been unconscious. They still needed confirmation, however, and JJ could see Ben's glance go to a narrow gap where the crumpled side door

of the van had been pushed in. It was probably fortunate that he was far too big to try
and enter the vehicle, JJ thought. Surely that
would be against any protocol for dealing
with a situation like this, anyway? What if
the van slid further, with someone inside?
That idea was enough to send a chill down
her spine.

'*Ow…*' Glenys cried out as she tried to turn
her head to look at her husband.

'What's hurting?' JJ reached through the
window to support the woman's head. 'Is it
your neck?'

'Yes… But only when I move.'

JJ palpated her neck carefully. 'Does this
hurt? Or this?'

'Ow…yes…that's really sore.'

'C six/seven,' JJ told Ben.

'Try and stay very still,' Ben told her. 'We're
going to put a collar on you to help look after
your neck. Is anything else hurting?'

'My…my arm…' Glenys groaned again.
'I can't move it…'

She was trying to move her head again to
look at her arm this time and JJ wasn't in a
good position to keep it steady. She found
herself eyeing up that gap in the side door.
She was a lot smaller than Ben.

'Would it be safe?' she asked quietly. 'To get inside?'

'Jack seemed to think things are stable,' Ben responded. 'It might move a bit with extra weight inside but it's not going to fall. It's got steel cables that will prevent that happening.'

JJ nodded. 'I'll see if I can get inside, then. I want to get that neck stabilised. And check on Derek.'

'Wait a bit. Someone will be down to help with that any minute,' Ben said. 'I think cutting that door clear and tipping the seat flat back will be the best way to get them out.'

But with every extra minute that passed, there was a chance that Glenys could try and move her neck again and, if she had a cervical fracture, it could make a huge difference to her outcome. It might even make the difference between life and death. And JJ could see that Ben was still trying to protect her and she didn't need to be taken care of right now.

She could do this.

A month or two ago the very idea of being confident to do something like this would have been a joke but, since then, she had created a new life for herself and she had become a new person along with that. She had a new name, even. Thanks to Cutler's Creek.

Thanks to Ben Marshall.

JJ edged sideways to reach the gap in the door. Because the van was tilted, she had to climb to get a foot through into the space.

'Watch out for sharp metal,' Ben warned. 'Take your time.'

Very slowly, JJ turned sideways and eased herself cautiously through the gap, freezing for a moment at the creak and screech of metal moving slightly against rock. The rope attached to her harness went tight, preventing her going further, so she unclipped it. She could hear Ben on his radio telling Mike what was going on. Then, as she steadied herself against an inbuilt table in the back of the van to move towards the front seats, she could hear the reassurance in Ben's voice as he spoke to Glenys.

'You've broken your arm, love,' he told her. 'That's why it's so sore. Can you feel me touching your hand here?'

'No.'

'What about here?'

'No... I can't feel anything except where it hurts.'

'We're going to give you something for

that pain. I just need to put a little needle in your other arm, okay?'

'But…but what about Derek? I can wait…' Glenys was breathing faster between groans and her level of distress was clearly increasing.

JJ was right behind the front seats now. She could lean forward to tilt Derek's head and open his airway. To feel his neck for a carotid pulse. The only thing she could feel, however, was Ben's intense gaze on her. She met his eyes and gave her head a tiny shake. There was nothing they could do for Derek.

Confirming such a huge loss for Glenys was not something JJ wanted to add to an already terrifying experience. A flash of memory came and went, leaving just a shadow of how hard it had been for her own grandmother to lose her life partner and how distressing those first shocking moments of realisation had been. She could see an echoing flash of understanding in Ben's gaze, as if he could read that thought and agreed that the awful news could wait, if possible. If Glenys didn't ask, either because she wasn't ready to know herself, or because she was distracted by her own situation?

'Okay, Glenys…' he said. 'I'm going to

slide this collar around your neck. Stay very still for me, okay?'

JJ held her head steady as Ben slipped the collar in place. She kept up a constant stream of reassurance for their patient but Glenys was crying now. Staying exactly where she was to hold Glenys's head still would have been a priority in any normal patient management but there were other things that needed to be done here. Like trying to get some vital signs.

'I've got a radial pulse on this side,' JJ told Ben. It wasn't possible to use a cuff and get a blood pressure reading but the fact that she could feel the pulse in the wrist meant that it wasn't low enough to be a concern. 'Heart rate's a hundred and four. Respirations twenty-two.'

'I can't get IV access on this arm,' Ben told her. 'Glenys has a displaced fracture of her radius and ulna and a dislocated elbow. Limb baselines absent in her hand so…we need some pain relief on board.'

JJ heard a lot more to that message. An absence of limb baselines meant that circulation was cut off to that hand and Glenys could lose it completely if the fracture wasn't realigned and the elbow joint relocated to prevent permanent damage to the brachial artery or nerves. This was an emergency and it would need more than simply pain relief. They were going to need some of the strongest medications they carried, like IV fentanyl and ketamine and midazolam that would pretty much knock Glenys out.

It also meant that IV access was essential and, if the arm that Ben could reach through the broken window was the injured one, access would have to be gained in the other arm. The one that JJ could reach through the gap in the front seats. Just as she was wondering how to prevent Glenys moving her neck, which could still cause damage even with the collar on, Ben leaned in to pass her a roll of tape.

'I'll put a dressing on that forehead laceration. Tape over it and round the headrest and that will keep everything still. We'll have to cut this safety belt but I don't want to do that until we're ready to get her out.' The seat belt was helping to hold Glenys still against the tilt of the van. 'I'm going to pass you the IV gear so you can get access on your side. You good with that?'

JJ nodded. She was more than good with that. She was in a space she excelled in now—with an urgent medical task to focus on. And, okay, this was an incredibly awkward space to be doing it in, compared with a nice, safe emergency department but that only made it an even more satisfying challenge to succeed in.

With a cannula safely in place and fluids running, JJ checked each ampoule that Ben had taped to the syringes he was passing her and, within only minutes, Glenys's level of distress had eased amazingly and she was sedated deeply enough to not be trying to move. It would still be painful to manipulate her broken arm and dislocated elbow but she wouldn't remember the procedure.

The awareness that her husband had probably died in this crash had also been temporarily paused and Glenys seemed to be totally unaware of the increased drama that was happening around her. A helicopter was hovering overhead and two firies were using cutting gear and a crowbar to remove the side door. At times the van was rocking enough to terrify JJ but she got through that by focusing completely on what she and Ben were doing. The awkwardness of this confined space made it very difficult for JJ to provide the counter-traction above the elbow so that Ben could pull the deformed bones and joint of Glenys's arm back into an alignment that would allow blood flow to resume and reduce ongoing nerve damage. By the time they had the arm splinted enough to keep it aligned, the back door of the van was gone. A paramedic with a stretcher was being winched down to join the rescue effort and the ledge around the crash site was becoming crowded.

'Come out, JJ. We've got this.'

'But what about getting some oxygen on? I want to check her breathing. And we need to have someone with a bag mask available.'

'I'm monitoring her. We can't get her out with you in there. It'll be very quick to winch the stretcher up.'

'We'll take her up to the road first.' The air rescue paramedic raised his voice to be heard over the sound of the helicopter rotors. 'We'll make sure she's stable before we transport her.' He was grinning at JJ. 'See you up there, Doc.'

There were several sets of hands to help JJ climb out of the van. A rope was clipped to her harness again and someone went with her as she climbed up to road level. She was only halfway up the long ladder as the stretcher carrying Glenys was lifted, with the paramedic holding it steady. The helicopter was so close JJ could feel the beat of the rotors right through to her bones. It was terrifying but exhilarating at the same time. She could understand completely the attraction that working with a team like this had for Ben. Every day would be an adrenaline rush. Every job serious enough to provide the kind of challenges that someone like Ben thrived on.

And he was certainly at his best right now, working with the air rescue team to make sure they hadn't missed any other injuries that Glenys had and that she was stable and as comfortable as possible for transport to a major hospital. The flight paramedics clearly knew Ben well and respected his skills and, although JJ had the medical seniority here, there was nothing she would have suggested be done any differently. She was proud of the confidence and competence that Ben was displaying. Still proud that he had referred to her as his 'partner' when he'd introduced her to Glenys.

Was it true that people came into your life for a reason? Standing back to watch what was happening gave JJ a moment to feel in-

credibly lucky to have met Ben Marshall.
Privileged to have been allowed as close as
she was to this man, even if it was only for
a brief time.

Because of the level of sedation she was
still under, Glenys was going to need careful monitoring.

'Want to come with us, Ben? Follow up on
what happens in the ED?'

He wanted to. Everyone could see just how
much he wanted to.

'Go,' Mike told him. 'Bruce and I can deal
with everything else that needs doing here.
We'll get the driver out and the road open
again. There's plenty of people who can get
the ambulance back to town and JJ will be
around for any emergencies, isn't that right,
Doc?'

JJ nodded. Firmly. Ben had given her
something amazing by including her in this
callout—a confidence in herself and her ability to tackle anything in life that she would
never, ever forget. She wanted to give something back.

Something that she knew could be just as
life changing for him—an opportunity to live
a dream of his, even if only for a brief time.

'Go,' she echoed Mike.

He didn't need telling again. They were already loading the stretcher into the helicopter down the road and Ben ran to catch up, ducking to keep well clear of the spinning rotors. He turned his head just before the clamshell doors cut off JJ's view and she saw his 'thumbs up' sign. She could almost feel the same thrill he was probably experiencing as the aircraft lifted and then swooped into the gorge to head off towards the city.

JJ could feel something else, as well. As if a part of her heart was in that helicopter with Ben and something was stretching tighter and tighter until it snapped.

And, suddenly, she felt very much alone even though she was still amongst a crowd of emergency service responders. It was only then that it really hit her. That she knew it was far more than just a suspicion that she was falling in love with Ben.

The helicopter was no more than a speck in the far distance now and it would vanish in a blink. That feeling was still there, however, and it wasn't just a part of her heart that was with Ben, was it? Without even realising it was happening, she seemed to have gifted him far too much of it.

It was a problem that would have to be dealt with at some point.

But not yet.

Please...not just yet.

# CHAPTER TEN

IF YOU LOOKED through the kitchen window of the small cottage that had become JJ's home in Cutler's Creek, you could see a rather overgrown vegetable garden between the house and barn on one side and a patch of grass on the other side, where Shaun the young sheep was creating a perfect circle around the post that anchored his long chain.

Just under the kitchen window was a rustic garden bench that was in a direct line with a wooden gate beneath an archway in the dense hedge that provided excellent protection for the cottage from any wind. Right now, it was also providing a very picturesque frame for the background of the spectacular mountain range and a sunset that was beginning to make both the sky and any last remaining winter snow on the peaks look as if they had just caught fire.

'How glorious is that?'

JJ let her breath out in a contented sigh. She was also letting go of a new sense of something poignant that came with being close to Ben. A feeling that time was running out? That she needed to make the most of every single moment?

'And how good is this?' She took a sip from the glass of white wine she was holding. 'Zac told me not to even think of doing any work tonight.'

'He told me the same thing.' Ben held up his bottle of lager in a toast. 'He's going to cover any callouts. He said we were local legends after that job last night and the least he could do was give us a proper night off.'

The lingering glance he gave JJ told her exactly what he thought a 'proper' night off should include and it was enough to take a curl of desire in her belly and make it explode into a heat as glorious as the deepening flames in the evening sky. It made it even easier to forget about that disturbing wobble she'd had when she'd seen Ben flying off into the distance yesterday.

Maybe the tensions of such a dramatic callout had led to her overly emotional reaction. She'd been able to get her head around it later. To remind herself that what they had between them had only ever been meant to be a temporary thing. Something fun. Something to make the most of. If she wanted to make it last just a little longer, she needed to remember that and that delicious curl of desire was more than enough to let her push aside any anxiety about any heartache the future might bring.

It would only take the tiniest encouragement—like running her tongue along her bottom lip, perhaps—and JJ knew that Ben would sweep her into his arms and carry her off to bed. And that would be heaven but she wanted to savour this moment, too. To stretch it out and revel in a connection with someone that went so much further than something that was only physical. They'd be able to stay friends, wouldn't they? Even if life pulled them in different directions?

'Local legends, huh?' JJ smiled. 'That might explain why so many people were tooting at me and waving when they drove past while I was out for a run with Shaun. Bruce even blipped his siren behind me, which nearly made me jump out of my skin.'

She had assumed it was just that she was becoming a local curiosity—the woman that went running with her pet lamb—but the idea that she had gained respect for her part in that dramatic cliff rescue yesterday felt... really good. As if her place in this community now had a solid foundation.

'I'm surprised you had the energy to go running. I was so tired I slept for the whole bus trip back from Dunedin.'

'It was more of a jog,' JJ admitted. 'Pretty much a walk on the way back. I felt a bit wrecked myself.'

'It was full on, all right.' It was Ben's turn to sigh and the sound was so satisfied that JJ knew he was smiling without looking. 'Possibly the best job ever.'

'Was it your first time in a helicopter?'

'Yep.' Ben wiped his mouth after taking a swig of his beer. 'Won't be the last, though, that's for sure. It was way better than anything I'd imagined. And I even got invited to go into Theatre and watch the surgery.'

'Zac told me. He said that Glenys did have a cervical fracture and it was a good thing we'd immobilised her neck early on.'

'The neurosurgeons did a posterior joint fusion with screws. Orthopaedics sorted her arm fracture and the elbow dislocation. She was in Theatre for hours. I had time to visit her this morning, though, before I got the bus back and she was doing well. She made me promise to say thank you for your help. Not that she remembered very much.'

'She must be devastated, knowing that the crash killed her husband.'

'Yes and no.' For a long moment Ben tilted his head back to look up at the sky where the colours were getting even more intense. JJ was caught by the poignant lines of his profile. And that the movement had exposed that soft, vulnerable skin just below his jawline. If she touched it with her fingers, or her lips, she would feel his pulse beating against her own skin. She was on the point of moving to do just that when Ben cleared his throat and spoke again.

'She said that she was going to miss him more than anyone could imagine but she was glad it had happened the way it did.'

'Really?'

'They both knew he had a bad heart and they'd wanted to make the most of whatever time they had left. A road trip around the South Island had been a dream of his for a very long time. It was a sudden death and he wouldn't have known anything about it, and he died living his dream. Glenys said she couldn't have wished for a better way for him to go.'

He was silent for another, long moment. 'Are we living our dreams, JJ?' he asked softly.

It was on the tip of her tongue to tell Ben what she was really thinking. That this was a dream for her. She was living in the most beautiful place she'd ever known. She had a job that allowed her to not only use all her skills but provided the challenge of learning many more. She was close enough to feel the warmth of a man she could very easily fall totally in love with if she let herself and she knew that, very soon, he would be taking her into his arms and stirring a passion that she just knew she would never find again in her lifetime.

Yes…she was living her dream. But it was one she would have to wake up from, wasn't it? Because Ben wasn't living his? He'd had a taste of what he really wanted to be doing with his life yesterday when he'd been working with the air rescue crew. But, then again, there was the way he'd looked at her only minutes ago. As if there was nothing more in the world he could want. Was she brave enough to try and find out whether he might have changed his mind about his 'type'? About *her*?

'Zac offered to sell me this cottage today,' she told Ben. 'Doc Donaldson is going to finally retire and he says there'll be a permanent job for me here if I want it.'

'Don's retiring?'

'He's excited about being a full-time grandpa. Liv came home today with baby Hugo and she's going to need lots of support, with Milly to look after, as well. She popped into the hospital on her way and you should have seen Betty. She was having to dry her eyes with her apron.'

'Do you think you'll stay?'

'I'm certainly going to give it a lot of thought.' JJ looked up at where the dramatic colour in the sky was fading into a much fainter pink. 'I'm happier here than I ever thought I would be. I actually feel like a completely different person than I was when I arrived.'

'I was just thinking that myself not so long ago.'

Ben's smile was so tender it almost hurt. JJ had to drop her gaze because it felt as if she might reveal far too much. There was something else she wanted to tell him, though.

'I rang my gran last night. Treating someone like Glenys who's the same sort of age always makes me think of her, of course, but I was also thinking about what I'd told you—that my parents' accident didn't bother me because I was too young to remember it.'

She could feel Ben's steady gaze on her. 'But it did?'

'Not in the way you might think. But I did start to wonder later how different my life might have been if they hadn't died. How different *I* might have been. I think my grandparents wrapped me up in cotton wool because they'd been so devastated that they'd lost their only child. I learned to be scared of anything that might hurt me and make them unhappy. In a different life, I might have been a lot braver.'

'You are brave.' Ben's voice was little more than a whisper. 'The woman that followed me down that ladder yesterday and climbed inside the back of a van that was being held up by rocks and a couple of steel cables is one of the bravest people I've ever met.'

There was a lump in JJ's throat as she finally met Ben's gaze, which threatened to stop her being able to breathe properly. Oh, dear Lord…she wasn't in danger of falling in love with this man, was she? The fall had already happened but the landing had been so painless she hadn't even noticed. She had to look away before Ben saw something that might make him run. Had to change the direction this conversation was going.

'My gran was so horrified when I told her about doing that.' JJ even managed a chuckle. 'She didn't quite say, "You're as bad as your mother," but I could hear her thinking it.'

Ben was smiling as he pulled her into his arms. 'I'd like to have met your mother,' he said. 'And I'm quite sure your dad adored her. But you do realise you might have grown up being called Journey, don't you?'

JJ was laughing now as he kissed her. 'You'd better make sure you don't break your promise.'

'What promise?'

'That my real name is our secret.'

'Why would I break it?'

'Because my gran has decided to come and see where I'm living. She's arriving next week. I suspect she wants to persuade me to go home to a place where camper vans don't drive off cliffs. She was the one who decided I had to be called by my middle name because my first name was so appalling so you'll have something in common. You just can't talk about it, that's all.'

But Ben was clearly thinking about something else as he kissed her again, his lips soft against hers, issuing an invitation JJ knew she had no hope of resisting any longer.

'Next week?' he murmured as he finally broke the kiss. 'That's only a few days away.'

'Mmm…'

JJ could still taste that kiss but she wanted more. She ran her tongue slowly over her bottom lip to capture the memory and, because she hadn't broken the eye contact with Ben, she could see the moment that passion ignited. She wrapped her arms around his neck as he got to his feet with her in his arms.

'We'd better make the most of having this place to ourselves, then, hadn't we?'

It wasn't that Ben was deliberately avoiding meeting JJ's grandmother when she came to Cutler's Creek the following week.

He was just busy, that was all.

As always, if he wasn't already up because of an emergency callout, he was out of bed the moment his alarm sounded, and he started several days a week with a workout that had evolved over the last year or two to become a fitness session for quite a few locals because there was no gym or instructors in town. He would meet Bruce and Mike and others in the local rugby field for a vigorous warmup and then a run, and by the time he'd showered and had his breakfast it was time to start work.

Normally, some days were very quiet compared to others but Ben preferred to be cruising around if that was the case, rather than sitting on station and twiddling his thumbs. He had a few regulars in town that he could check on, like Albert Flewellan, who was still getting used to having a home oxygen supply and monitoring his lung function, and Bert, who was almost as old as Albie and had angina that had been stable for years but he still needed reminding to use his GTN spray before he started mowing his lawns or digging the vegetable garden to avoid a frightening episode of chest pain that required an emergency ambulance call. If Mike or some of the other guys were at the fire station, it was good to call in there as well to have a yarn and plan some new training sessions.

This week, however, Ben didn't have to employ his usual strategies to stave off the slightest hint of boredom because there seemed to be a sudden spike in callouts. An eight-year-old boy had fallen out of a tree in the school playground and given himself concussion. Two girls came off their ponies when they were out for a ride and one of them had broken her wrist. He had a hypoglycaemic episode of a young diabetic man and a long trip to a farm on the edge of the area he covered to a nasty accident where a farm bike had rolled on a hill. The helicopter had had to be called in for that job and Ben had been away from town for the whole afternoon.

He'd almost forgotten that JJ's mother was *in* town, in fact, when he spotted an elderly woman on the other side of the road from the ambulance station when he drove in after a cruising session on Friday afternoon. He knew she wasn't local, of course, but Cutler's Creek was a picturesque enough country town to persuade tourists to stop for a while. They liked to take pictures of the old, stone church, read the names on the war memorial in the main street or have lunch in the beer garden at the pub. Not many of them wandered as far as the ambulance station, though, or stopped to sit on the bench seat that happened to be there because it had once been a bus stop.

Ben parked the ambulance in the garage and wandered across the road. 'Are you all right, love?' he asked. 'Not lost, are you?'

'No… I'm just out for a walk. I thought I'd go and have a look at that gift shop I went past the other day.'

'The Crafty Corner?' Ben smiled. 'It's well worth a visit. People around these parts still knit tea cosies.'

'It's a bit further than I thought it would be.' The woman sighed. 'I just stopped to give my feet a bit of a rest.'

'How far have you come?'

'From the hospital.'

'That's quite a walk.' Ben was looking at the woman more carefully now. 'You weren't there because you were sick, were you?'

'Oh, no… I went out to lunch with Dr Donaldson and I was just filling in time until my granddaughter finished her work and we could go home.'

Finally, Ben clicked. 'You're JJ's grandmother, aren't you? Pleased to meet you. I'm Ben.' Would JJ have said anything to her grandmother about him? About *them*? No. Ben brushed the thought away. Why would she? It wasn't as if they were in the kind of relationship where you got introduced to family members.

'I'm Shona Hamilton.' The look Ben was getting made him feel as if he'd misbehaved in some way. 'Why on earth does everyone here call her "JJ"? What's wrong with being called "Joy"?'

'Nothing at all.' Ben couldn't help his grin as he lowered his voice to a conspiratorial whisper. 'It's a lot better than being called "Journey", though, isn't it?'

Shona Hamilton's eyes widened and then narrowed into a sharp gaze.

'Joy never tells anybody her real name. How did you find out?'

'Can't say,' Ben said. 'I'm sworn to secrecy and I'm an extremely trustworthy person.'

Shona's face softened into the kind of creases only a woman in their eighties can collect and her smile was slow and genuine.

'I think I like you, Ben Marshall,' she said. 'We'll keep this our little secret, too, shall we?'

'No worries. Now, would you like me to get you a glass of water? Or take you into town in my ambulance to save your feet?'

'No, no... I'll just sit here for a moment

longer and I'll be absolutely fine. It's not exactly a hardship, is it, with that amazing view of the mountains? I'm starting to understand why Joy loves this place so much. Did you know she's thinking of staying here for ever?'

'I did hear that she was thinking about it.'

'That charming Dr Donaldson told me at lunch that they're very much hoping to persuade her to stay. He even suggested me moving here myself. Can you imagine that?'

Actually, Ben could imagine that. Shona Hamilton would fit right in amongst the older characters in this community and it would be the perfect place to spend the last years of one's life. He would probably drift back here to live himself, sometime in the future, when he'd had his fill of adventures. Who wouldn't want to sit on a bench like this, on a quiet street, soaking up the sheer pleasure of looking at mountain peaks like theirs?

He and his nan used to sit like this, at the top of the steps on the edge of their veranda, and they'd gaze at a very similar mountain view. His earliest memories were of being cuddled in her lap as she'd sat and watched a sunset but, as he'd got older, they would sit side by side. They wouldn't say much, if anything at all. He'd lean his head on her shoulder, even when he'd got to be a teenager and would have died of embarrassment if any of his mates had seen him, because that had been his happy place. His refuge. The place where he'd known he was loved the most by the person *he* loved the most. His nan. The one person who had ever really wanted him.

He'd missed sitting with her, so, so much. He'd only been fifteen when she'd died suddenly but his mother had been living in Australia for years by then. She'd sold his nan's house and used the money to pack him off to a boarding school and then university so that she could finally abdicate a responsibility she'd never wanted in the first place.

And here he was, with someone who was about the same age as his nan would have been, and she wasn't someone familiar enough to have been slotted somewhere safe, like into the compartment of a patient he could focus on treating or someone who had a clearly defined role, like Betty at the hospital. To him, Shona was JJ's grandma. Someone who'd raised a child of *her* child.

Just like his nan.

And…and Ben could feel a lump in his throat that he'd never sat still long enough to feel since…for ever ago. Since he'd been about fifteen, in fact. He couldn't sit still any longer, either. He was on his feet before he'd even processed the thought.

'I'll have to go,' he said. 'There's a patient I forgot to check on when I was out and about before. Are you sure I can't drop you into town? Or back at the hospital, maybe?'

'No, thanks, love. I can manage the rest of the walk into town and Joy will come and pick me up when she's finished work.' She got to her feet, picking up an old-fashioned handbag from the seat beside her and Ben realised she was just about as short as his nan had been. The white curls on Shona's head barely reached above his elbow. She was smiling up at him. 'Don't forget…' she warned.

'Forget what?' Ben was already moving—the need to find something to distract himself almost overwhelming.

'Our little secret.' Shona tapped her nose. 'About Joy…?' Her smile widened as Ben turned back. 'Or perhaps I should remember to say JJ? I get the feeling she likes her new name as much as this place and all her new friends.' Already faded blue eyes were looking distinctly misty now. 'I worry about her. I always have and always will. But she's happy and that's all you ever want for someone you love, isn't it?'

'So… I hear you met my gran the other day?'

'It was supposed to be our little secret.' Ben put the newspaper wrapped parcel of fish and chips he had picked up from Cutler's Creek's only takeaway on the kitchen bench of JJ's cottage. 'It's a thing I have with Hamilton women.'

JJ laughed. 'You certainly made an impression. She only told me about meeting you when we were on our way to Queenstown this afternoon so she could get her flight home. She said you were a very "charming young man".'

'And did you agree with her?' Ben was smiling down at JJ, loving the way she held his glance, her eyes dancing with amusement—or perhaps just the pleasure of seeing him again.

'I didn't dare say anything. I think she guessed that there was something going on between us. I don't think she would have believed me if I'd told her we were just good friends, so it was safer not to say anything.'

The shaft of disappointment that JJ would

describe their connection as simply a friendship came from nowhere. Or maybe it went deeper than that and it was a fear that he might be missing out on something important in life but, whatever it was, it had no right to appear at all. It wasn't as if Ben wanted anything more than a good friendship with JJ. Heaven forbid…he had always run a mile when any woman had got 'serious'. The beat of silence between them made him think he was expected to say something himself but JJ was still smiling up at him and she was the one who broke the silence.

'She liked you a lot. Which is possibly why she warned me off.'

'What?' Ben's eyebrows shot up. 'And there I was thinking we'd bonded for life, your gran and me.'

JJ was laughing. 'She said she suspected you were a "bit wild".'

'A bit wild, huh?' Ben pulled JJ closer.

It had been too long since he'd kissed this woman, what with her having a visitor in the cottage all week. And what better way to dismiss that odd feeling that he might be missing out on anything. This was everything that any man could possibly want—a gorgeous woman and the best sex ever with no strings attached.

An almost desperate desire to sink into that delicious distraction didn't mean he couldn't take his time, though, with a gentle, teasing touch of his lips on hers. A tiny flick of his tongue on her lower lip as she pressed closer, her body melting against his as she wrapped her arms around his neck. He loved the way she did that. And the way her eyes drifted shut as she tilted her head back, as though all she wanted to focus on was this moment.

This kiss...

If he turned up the heat, they would be in her bed in no time flat. How was it that he'd completely lost track of how many times they'd made love over the last weeks but it still felt just as thrilling as that very first time in that mountain hut? No, that wasn't quite true, was it? It felt *better*. Just as exciting but there was a different dimension to it that he couldn't quite name. Safety, perhaps? Because they knew each other's bodies so intimately now but, instead of creating boundaries, it provided a foundation that was safe enough to keep exploring. To find a new touch or rhythm or level of closeness that seemed to suggest being with JJ could never, ever get boring.

Maybe *trust* was the word he was looking for?

Not that an accurate analysis was needed. Ben just knew how to play the heat level like a well-tuned instrument now and a crescendo would be all the more satisfying if they waited a while to enjoy the anticipation. Besides, he'd missed lunch today.

'I'm starving,' he confessed, breaking the kiss before desire could obliterate anything other physical need. 'And I'd hate for Cutler's Creek's best battered cod and chips to go soggy.'

JJ's hand slid from his neck to the front of his chest and pushed gently as if she needed a boost to move away from him. 'Make some space on the table,' she told him. 'I'll get the bread and butter so you can have your chippie sandwiches.'

The pile of stuff on the table suggested that JJ had had trouble finding something in her shoulder bag. It reminded Ben of that first day he'd met her and how he'd known how rattled she'd been because she was a neat freak but she'd just emptied the contents of her bag onto the table. He'd also known that he had been the one to help push her well out of any comfort zone by arriving with that lamb in the box.

He would have taken it away again if he'd thought she couldn't cope—he'd just wanted to tease her a bit. In retrospect, however, he knew that he'd liked being the reason she'd been rattled. He'd teased her because it had been a safe way to play with what was a totally inappropriate attraction. He might have believed he didn't want anything to do with the new locum doctor on a personal level but, deep down, his body—or soul—had recognised something very different.

There was an old, lumpy envelope amongst the collection of things like hand cream and tissue packs and a lipstick or two. It wasn't sealed so he could see that it was stuffed full of photographs as he picked it up. JJ reached past him to put down the board with a mound of freshly sliced bread.

'Gran gave me those. At the airport. She said she thought I might need some family stuff around if I'm wondering whether to stay here for ever.'

'May I look?'

JJ's eyebrows rose. 'You're asking permission?'

'It's a private sort of thing.'

'Oh…yeah…like a passport?'

So he wasn't the only one to get flashbacks of the first time they'd met? Interesting… There was no reprimand in JJ's tone, however. It was more like a private joke about what had led to a pact to keep a secret. That first baby step they'd taken towards a connection, and a friendship that might not be 'serious' but it was certainly more significant than anything Ben had ever experienced before in his life.

Because…yes…*trust* was the word he'd been searching for.

They trusted each other. They were on the same page about enjoying what they had together with no expectations of anything permanent. Quite the opposite, in fact, and maybe that was why it was always so good to be together, because they were both making the most of every moment while it lasted.

It was a rare night off for both of them at the same time so they opened a bottle of wine. Ben flattened chunky pieces of fried potato between his slices of buttered bread and they broke off generous servings of delicious fish fillets in crispy batter to eat with their fingers. They had to wipe their hands as they spread the photographs from the envelope over the table in front of them.

'Most of these I've never seen,' JJ told Ben. 'They were part of the only belongings that got packed up and taken back to New Zealand when my grandparents came to get me—and my father's body. Gran said she was sorry. She should have given them to me long ago.'

'What happened to your mother's body?'

'She's buried somewhere in the south of France. I got the impression that her family blamed my father for the accident as much as my family blamed her.'

'So you've never met your mother's family?'

JJ shook her head. 'I've always wanted to go but…well, I knew how much it would upset my grandparents. Even falling off my pony when I was seven frightened Gran so much I stopped my riding lessons and that was my favourite thing to be doing.' She shook her head. 'And, yeah… I know it's a bit pathetic but I was so focused on med school and then life just got so busy and… I just haven't made it to the other side of the world yet. One day…'

Ben stilled for a moment, his heart giving

a peculiar squeeze. The words were on the tip of his tongue but something stopped him from saying them aloud.

*We could do that one day... I'll come with you... It'd be fun, wouldn't it?*

Maybe it was that squeeze tightening a notch or two that squashed the words so they didn't emerge. He couldn't make a promise he might not be able to keep because he would hate himself if he hurt someone who was such a genuinely *nice* person. He could imagine JJ as a small girl, taking on the responsibility of trying to keep her grandmother happy because she cared that much. Enough to make sure she followed all the rules and kept herself and the people she loved as safe as she possibly could.

But there was another part of the real JJ, wasn't there? And maybe Ben was the first person to have seen the brave, adventurous side of her. Looking at these old snapshots of a young couple making the most of life—plastered with tomatoes in La Tomitina festival in Spain, dancing in the rain at Glastonbury, walking in a lavender field in Provence—he could see who she'd probably inherited her adventurous streak from. She was definitely her mother's daughter.

'Your gran would have said your mum was a "bit wild", too, I guess?'

'Oh, absolutely. It was the biggest reprimand I could get as a kid. Nobody had to say it. They'd just look at me—sort of surprised and disappointed at the same time—and I'd know they were thinking that I was just like my mother and that it wasn't a good thing to be.'

'You look so like her.' Ben wiped his fingers again and then picked up the photograph of her parents dancing in the rain. With drooping flowers in her waist-length dark hair that was loose and totally soaked, wearing denim dungarees with nothing but a bra beneath them, she must have been frozen but he'd never seen such a look of joy on someone's face as she looked up at the tall, young man whose hands she was holding. And he was looking just as happy. Just as utterly in love with life and the person he'd found to share it with.

'I probably *was* conceived at that festival.' JJ was grinning. 'You were spot on when you guessed but I didn't want to give you the satisfaction of being right.'

'Is that where they met?'

'Yes. My father had gone to a conference in

London. He'd just finished his double degree with honours—in law and accountancy—and my grandfather had already changed the letterhead for his legal firm to be Hamilton and Hamilton but some people he met at the conference were going to the festival for the weekend and he got invited to tag along. My mum, Celine, was singing there and they somehow met each other and that was that. My dad…never came back. I'm sure he meant to. Eventually.'

'I'm not surprised they wanted time to just be together,' Ben said softly. 'They look so much in love.'

'They do, don't they? I like to think that they were that happy. It's not something everyone finds in life, is it?'

There was an odd note in JJ's voice. Something so poignant it brought a lump to Ben's throat and made him want to offer comfort. To tell her that she would find that kind of love one day herself. Why wouldn't she? Who wouldn't want to be with someone as beautiful and intelligent and courageous as JJ?

She was gathering up the photographs now. Stuffing them back into that old envelope. And then she started clearing the table and Ben could recognise that need to be busy to stop thinking about something that caused some kind of pain and he knew he could help.

He knew exactly how to distract JJ. And, as a bonus, it was exactly what he wanted most in the world himself right now. He got to his feet and went to where she was standing in front of the sink. He turned off the tap and took the dish brush out of her hands. Without saying anything, he smoothed tiny, stray tresses of hair away from her face and then held her head between his hands as he bent to kiss her.

And, this time, the gentle teasing with his lips and tongue swiftly morphed into something that both offered and demanded complete focus. He meant business, and, when he slid his hands down the length of JJ's body a minute or two later to pull her hips closer to his own, she would be in no doubt what that business was all about. It seemed like she more than welcomed the distraction and the task of tidying up and washing plates was abandoned without a second thought for either of them. It could wait. Until the morning, even, because Ben couldn't imagine wanting to leave JJ's bed any time soon.

There was only so long that even the most passionate lovemaking could last, mind you, and at some point considerably later Ben found himself with JJ in his arms, feeling her heart rate slowly decrease and hearing her breathing return to a resting soft sigh. Her skin was warm against his. His lips were being tickled by her hair as he pressed a kiss to her head and the scent of her was filling his nostrils. She was so quiet that Ben wondered if she was falling asleep but her muscle tone told him that she was still awake. She was just…being with him…

Slowly—so slowly that Ben hardly noticed it happening—he could feel himself slipping into a space that he'd been reminded of very recently thanks to that encounter with JJ's grandmother.

That space of just being with someone that you loved and that you were loved *by*. A sense that all was right with the world. That pure joy could be as simple as just sitting still with that person. Being *with* them… body and soul…

It was why Ben had never let himself sit still ever since his nan had died, wasn't it? Because, if he did, he would remember how it felt to love and be loved like that. And he would have to remember the devastation of losing that kind of love. He'd never let himself get close enough to anyone to be in danger of facing that kind of loss ever again but...

But he was in very real danger of falling in love with JJ Hamilton.

He could feel it hovering. A force that had the power to push him over that particular cliff and create the fall. And he couldn't let it happen because he would lose before he'd even attempted to win. This had never been meant to happen. Part of that trust he had with JJ was because he'd felt safe. Had that feeling of safety meant that he'd let down his guard and that closeness had grown without him even noticing it?

But neither of them were anything like each other's 'type' and they'd both agreed they were incompatible and it could never work long term. JJ had made it crystal clear that this connection was only temporary and he'd been totally on board. He just had to live up to his end of the bargain, now. For both their sakes. And, for the sake of a friendship that they might be able to keep for ever, if he didn't ruin it by suggesting it could be something more.

So much more, it felt like it could be everything—more than he'd ever had before, and that was a terrifying thought because he already knew what it was like to lose something huge. How hard it had been to build a new life and to find something that he could be passionate about but still keep himself safe. He'd found that in his work. Never in a person because he knew when he was stepping into dangerous territory and he knew so well how to retreat or change direction, it had become automatic. How had he ventured further than ever before into that forbidden space without an alarm sounding?

It was sounding now, however, loudly enough to scare Ben into action despite it feeling oddly hard to breathe suddenly and that it was taking an astonishing amount of effort to force his body to move.

He pressed another kiss to JJ's hair. Took another breath just to drink in what he knew was going to be the last intimate scent of this amazing woman.

'Gotta go,' he whispered. 'Early start tomorrow.'

'Okay…'

He knew JJ was watching him as he pulled his clothes back on but he didn't turn back.

Not until he was at her bedroom door and even then it was only for a heartbeat.

''Night, JJ... Sleep well...'

# CHAPTER ELEVEN

IT HAD BEEN the most perfect night of JJ's life.

She had woken up the next morning knowing that something had changed. Something amazing. Something that had the promise of making the rest of her life as perfect as it could possibly be?

She was still thinking about it when she went to give Shaun his container full of sheep nuts for breakfast, just as the sun was rising and the first light was kissing the mountaintops in the distance with a promise of it becoming a glorious spring morning. How could it not be a gorgeous day when it felt like JJ was floating an inch or two off the ground? Happier than she'd ever felt in her life?

That moment, when Ben had tried to protect her from dealing with the camper van crash and she'd felt that touch on her soul that had warned her that she was falling in love with him had been one-sided. Last night had made her feel as if there was more to it than simply a touch. That there was a kind of filament attached to that place that had been touched and it was being held on the other end by Ben. She could believe that what she was feeling wasn't one-sided any longer. He might not be ready to accept it, but it was there.

Maybe it had been something in his eyes when she'd told him that her grandmother was suspicious there was something more than friendship going on between them—as if he wanted that to be true but was afraid of admitting it? It had been her turn to feel protective then, and it had been no hardship to respond to that… oh, so distracting kiss.

Or perhaps it had happened when he'd been looking at that photo. That note in his voice when he'd commented on how much in love her parents looked had almost brought her to tears. She could hear a poignancy that suggested he was looking at perfection in a relationship that he never expected to find for himself.

Maybe JJ hadn't expected it, either. She most certainly hadn't expected to find it with someone like Ben Marshall—the kind of rule-bending, charismatic, maverick bad boy that she'd been brought up to believe that getting too close to would only lead to trouble. Or worse…

But wasn't that exactly how she'd found what she'd been searching for?

This chapter of JJ's life had all begun because her relationship with Ian had died a natural death. Because he'd let her know that she was possibly the most boring person on earth. Because she'd been left wondering if was doing something wrong in the way she was living her life and that she might be missing out on something that was very, very important. As crucial as the real meaning of life, even?

Coming to Cutler's Creek had indeed changed her life. Changed *her*. Or, rather, meeting Ben Marshall had.

He'd given her a new name right from the start which, with the benefit of hindsight, JJ could see as pretty much an invitation to discover who she really was. Joy, the good girl? Or JJ, who might actually be a bit wild and adventurous, just like her mother had been?

He'd challenged her, physically and emotionally, to get fitter and to learn new things that she'd never considered relevant before. To become at least a more interesting person, if not a markedly better version of herself.

And he'd shown her what passion was all about. More than ever before in her life, JJ was missing having a mother. No, not 'a' mother. *Her* mother. So that she could have talked about how she was feeling right now with someone who had, apparently, lived life in a way that gave her the kind of joy—and love—that was precisely what JJ had feared she'd was never going to experience.

Talking to Shaun the sheep wasn't going to be helpful in any way at all but JJ found herself doing it anyway. Perhaps it made how she was feeling more real by hearing the words spoken aloud?

'I'm in love with him,' she told Shaun, as she moved his post so that he could enjoy fresh grass for the day. 'Yeah… I know he's a bad boy but, you know what?'

Shaun nudged her hand, looking for more food, but JJ pretended it was because he wanted the answer to that question. She was smiling as she leaned closer, checking that his collar was comfortable.

'I reckon I've got a bit of bad girl in me. Deep down and you know what *that* means?'

Shaun had started eating grass. He wasn't interested, but JJ was going to tell him anyway. Because she had to tell someone.

'It means we're soul mates. And I think that Ben knows that, too. He just needs a bit of time to get used to the idea.'

Yes…it had been the most perfect night. Or *almost* the most perfect night because it would have been even better if she'd fallen asleep in Ben's arms and they'd woken up together this morning. That didn't really bother her because he'd never stayed a whole night. Yet. He probably thought he was protecting her reputation in Cutler's Creek or that he didn't want to disturb her sleep with the kind of pre-dawn start that let him have a workout with his fitness group before starting a shift at the ambulance station at seven a.m.

Maybe that was why JJ didn't see it coming. And why what happened only a couple of days later was so shocking.

He hadn't intended to tell her like this, in front of a whole bunch of people.

It just happened.

Because he'd only had the phone call the evening before and all the people who needed to know what was about to happen were all in the same place at the same time.

Cutler's Creek Hospital's kitchen.

Betty had outdone herself making a morning tea to welcome Zac Cameron back to work full time and to celebrate his family being together again. His gorgeous wife, Liv, had baby Hugo in her arms and the adorable two-year-old Milly was being held up by her grandfather so that she could choose a treat from the laden table.

'What about a lamington, Milly? Or a sausage roll?'

'No. *That* one…' A small finger was pointing to a platter right in front of Ben.

'A girl after my own heart.' Ben picked up two warm triangles of cheese toastie. 'Here you go, sweetheart. One for you and one for me.'

The staff on duty, including nurses, cleaners and the receptionist, were balancing cups of tea and paper serviettes laden with food but there were lots of other people as well, like Bruce and Mike and many of the volunteers that gave their time to both the ambulance and fire services. Don Donaldson, the man who'd followed in his father's footsteps as the local doctor and who'd kept Cutler's

Creek Hospital going despite threats of closure, had just given a speech to welcome Zac back and to express his profound relief that their family was reunited.

'I never dreamed my life could be this wonderful,' he told everyone. 'All those years ago I thought I'd hit the jackpot, just getting a locum to come to Cutler's Creek for a while, when Zac arrived here. I never thought he'd bring my daughter back into my life, let alone start a whole new chapter of the Donaldson family's story. I nearly didn't get to live to see it, mind you, with that bit of drama that put me out of action for a while but that only makes it all the more precious. All I need now is to find my replacement so that the next party we have will be to celebrate a *real* retirement. None of this part-time nonsense, no matter how much I enjoy working with you all.'

He was looking at JJ as he spoke, his smile teasing, but everybody knew there was a genuine plea there. They all knew that the offer had been made and that JJ had promised to think about it and they were all hoping she would choose to stay. Ben agreed with the consensus. JJ was perfect for Cutler's Creek.

Dedicated, clever and courageous. A brilliant doctor who would only become more and more of a vital part of this community in general and the emergency services branch of it in particular. It was just a damn shame he wouldn't be here to watch that happen.

This was the first time Ben had seen her since the night he'd taken the fish and chip dinner to her cottage. The place he'd ended up being oddly desperate to escape from. It had been a lot more difficult to escape from that background need to keep moving and stay well clear of that disturbing kind of stillness that had prompted him to leave her bed that night but the perfect opportunity to prevent him possibly ever being that still again had presented itself only last night.

The chance to live his dream.

JJ's head turned, as if she could feel Ben watching her as Don Donaldson was finishing his speech, and the instant her gaze met his, Ben knew she could see something in his expression—or perhaps even read his mind—and she was suddenly confused. Bewildered, even? Had she been seeking encouragement to commit to the job here and being a part of Cutler's Creek permanently but she had picked up the vibe that he wasn't going to be here himself?

Everybody was waiting for JJ to respond in some way and Ben could sense her hesitation. He could understand it, too. She was standing at a rather significant crossroad in her life at this moment and it was a huge decision. One that he didn't think she should be forced to make in public, like this, which gave him an urge to protect her. To deflect the attention and give her some time to collect herself.

He did realise that it might not be the kindest way to tell her his news but it was certainly the easiest. Possibly the only way, because if he was alone with JJ and close enough to touch her, he might have changed his mind and taken a chance on a very different direction in his own life.

'I have a bit of an announcement myself,' he said aloud.

Every head turned in his direction. Except for JJ, who dropped her gaze, as if she knew she might need a moment of relative privacy.

'I had a call last night,' Ben told them. 'One of the guys on the helicopter crew in Dunedin had an accident on his motorbike and he'll be out of action for some time. I've been offered a spot to train and work with the crew.'

He'd certainly made himself the centre of attention instead of JJ. Mike was beaming.

'Wow…you've had your heart set on that for a long time, mate. Congratulations.'

But Zac was looking dismayed. 'You're going to be missed around here. What will we do without you?'

'There's a locum paramedic from Invercargill who'll fill in until a permanent station manager can be found but, hey, you guys—and the volunteers on the team—can manage anything yourselves, you know. I can just drop in and do the transport.'

Betty was scowling. 'When?' she demanded. 'When are you leaving?'

'Um…it's short notice. I'm sorry. I'm hoping to head out of town by the day after tomorrow.'

The silence that followed his admission was broken only by whimpers from baby Hugo. People were exchanging glances and Ben was taken aback by the wave of emotion he could feel in this room.

Had he become a more integral part of this community than he'd realised? In his need to keep moving and his instant acceptance of the job offer, he hadn't really factored in that he was going to hurt people that he cared about. A lot. He was going to miss them as much, if not more than they would miss him.

He was giving up the place that had been his home for several years.

He was giving up friends. The kind of friends that would have always had his back, no matter what, just as he would have had theirs.

He was giving up JJ.

The silence grew. So did the lump in Ben's throat. But then someone spoke. Clearly enough that perhaps it was only Ben who could pick the note of courage beneath the words.

'Seeing as it's the morning for announcements,' JJ said, 'I'd like you all to know that I'm going to accept the permanent position that I've been offered here at Cutler's Creek. You can be as much of a full-time grandpa as you want, Don, and enjoy more time with Jill. And, Zac? Let's talk about that cottage later. I think Shaun and I will be very happy to make it our home for the foreseeable future.'

The atmosphere in the kitchen did a rollercoaster swoop and any upset about Ben's departure seemed to have been forgotten in the very real delight that JJ had decided to stay. He was as delighted as anybody. He was also proud of her. She'd come a very long way since he'd knocked her off her feet on the side of the road. She'd not only made herself a part of this community, she seemed to have found her feet and a confidence in what she wanted in her life.

JJ Hamilton was going to be fine, even if he wasn't going to be around to look after her, and knowing that was probably going to make it a little easier to leave. Ben was still relieved that he wasn't going to have too much time to think about it, though. No time at all, really, given the amount of packing and organisation he had to have done by tomorrow.

He needed to get on with that, in fact, so he shouldn't be standing around here drinking coffee and eating Betty's cheese toasties. The noise level in the kitchen was increasing rapidly with people gathering around JJ, eager to tell her and each other how happy they were that she wasn't going anywhere.

Nobody noticed when Ben slipped quietly from the room.

\* \* \*

He'd told her that she was one of the bravest people he'd ever met.

She was certainly a very different person from the one who'd arrived in Cutler's Creek, looking for time out from a life that she hadn't been sure she'd been happy with, and JJ knew she had Ben to thank for the new version of herself that she'd grown into.

However hard it was going to be to get used to not having Ben Marshall in her life, she would always be thankful that she'd met this amazing person and perhaps the best way she could show him how much he meant to her was to give all the encouragement she could so that he could find exactly what he wanted from life.

Maybe that was why she found more courage than ever at that moment and had made a choice that was a public confirmation of the new person she had become. Someone who recognised what the most important things in her life were and that was…belonging. Caring about something to the point of passion, and that didn't necessarily have to be a particular person, did it? It could be a profession with new facets to her work—like a qualification in mountain rescue. A community that had more than its share of warm-hearted, generous people. A small, rural hospital, even, that offered such a variety of work and skill levels required that it would never get boring.

It took even more courage, however, to keep smiling when she'd seen Ben walking out of those kitchen doors—out of the perfect life that she'd been dreaming about only in the last day or two—and JJ knew that it might take a long time for her to be able to remember that moment without a pain that was sharp enough to make her catch her breath every single time.

She wasn't wrong.

In some ways, it actually got worse. For the first few days, that included saying goodbye to Ben, wishing him all the best and exchanging promises to keep in touch. Pushing that pain to one side was necessary to simply keep functioning. That the first couple of weeks without him were so busy also helped keep it at bay. Having negotiated the purchase price of Zac's cottage, a few visits to Queenstown had to be slotted into her timetable to talk to her bank manager and arrange for a solicitor to draw up the sales agreement and there were plenty of other things to think about, too.

'That big paddock through the gate in the hedge is yours,' Zac warned JJ. 'It needs a bit of managing. I've been getting Greg to mow it for hay every summer and he runs a mob of sheep on it occasionally to keep it down but you might want to use it for something else. There used to be a Clydesdale horse there, called Chloe, who kind of came with the property. Greg's looking after her on his farm at the moment but I'm sure she'd love to come back to her old paddock. She'd be great company for that pet sheep of yours.'

'I'll think about it,' JJ promised. 'I need the contact details for the septic tank company, too. And that hedge cutting firm. Oh... and I'll need to get some firewood in so that it's dry for next winter, too, won't I?'

Cutler's Creek's temporary ambulance station manager, Trevor, was doing his part to keep JJ busier than usual. A perfectly pleasant man in his late fifties, Trevor was an EMT rather than a paramedic but he was keen to provide the best service he could at his lower skill level. JJ was determined to do *her* best as well and not to make negative comparisons to Ben but it wasn't easy, especially after she noticed on his first visit to the hospital that Trevor carried a notebook version of ambulance protocols in a pocket of his uniform and referred to them frequently.

It made JJ realise how she must have seemed to Ben when he'd come into the hospital that day and found she'd labelled practically every single item and cupboard in their treatment room/emergency department. It seemed like a lifetime ago that she'd needed to follow rules so rigidly to feel safe but, at the same time, it was so patently obvious that they were such different people. How had she been so sure she'd found the person who was her soul mate? And why was she now living with an emptiness that made her so sure she was never going to meet anyone else she felt like that about?

With Zac's family responsibilities including a very precious, tiny baby, it had been easy to persuade him to let JJ be first on call—day or night—for any ambulance call-outs for potential medical or trauma emergencies that might need a doctor attending. With Trevor's skill level combined with his determination to follow every guideline and to err on the side of caution those calls for backup were coming in often enough to add noticeably to her workload.

There was a dislocated finger on the rugby field on a Saturday morning and an urgent call to a suspected heart attack later the same day, but it turned out that Bert had, once again, forgotten to use his GTN spray before doing something a bit more energetic. The call to a woman in labour a couple of days after that had both JJ and Debbie responding to meet the ambulance at a farm well out of town, but that also turned out to be a false alarm. The woman, who was visiting her aunt, was most likely experiencing her first Braxton-Hicks contractions and they had both panicked.

'I miss Ben,' Debbie said as they drove back to the hospital, now well behind in everything else that needed to be done that afternoon. 'Even if she'd been well into second stage labour, he would have probably just delivered the baby and turned up at the hospital with them both.'

JJ simply nodded her agreement. She and Debbie had become good friends but she couldn't admit just how deeply she was missing Ben. Because talking about it not only wouldn't help, it could, quite easily, make it a whole lot worse.

'Do you think he made the right decision? To leave?'

'I think we all have to do what's best for us. You only get one life, don't you, and you have to follow your dreams.'

'And you think you've made the right decision? To stay here?'

'I love it here.' JJ nodded again, more enthusiastically this time. 'I'm still getting surprised by how much. D'you know, I told Zac the other day that I needed to know where to order firewood from so I can get a supply in before next winter and I got home from work yesterday to find that someone had dumped a trailer load of cut wood in front of the barn. I have no idea who. That's not something that would have ever happened anywhere else I've lived.'

Debbie had turned to watch the countryside rolling past from the side window. 'I'm glad you're happy here. I hope Ben's happy in his new job, too. No... I take that back.' Her sideways smile was mischievous. 'I hope he *hates* his new job and comes back here before anyone permanent gets appointed to our station.'

'I suspect he's very happy,' JJ said quietly. 'One of these days, he'll drop in wearing his flight suit and helmet with the biggest smile on his face we've ever seen.'

When she had reason to summon the rescue helicopter only a week or so later, she watched it land on the road close to where she was stabilising a young man who'd come off his motorcycle at high speed and her heart was pounding. Was that Ben at one end of the stretcher, stooping to move beneath rotors that would keep spinning so they could take off within minutes to get this critically injured patient to a major trauma centre?

Any disappointment that Ben wasn't part of the crew was easily dismissed until the handover of her patient was complete and the air rescue crew was ready to load the stretcher back into the helicopter. It was only then that JJ couldn't stop herself asking.

'How's Ben? I… I thought I might see him today…'

'He's up in Christchurch for a couple of days. Doing a HUET course.'

'HUET?'

'Helicopter Underwater Escape Training.'

JJ's eyes widened. She could only imagine how much of an adrenaline rush learning to deal with a time-critical emergency like that would be. 'Wow…he must be loving that.'

The crew was already moving now but the paramedic turned to grin at JJ. 'If anybody was born to do this job, it's Ben. You'll see him soon.'

In a way, knowing that she was very likely to see him soon made JJ miss him even more. How hard was it going to be, that first time, to see that he had made totally the right decision and that he was loving his new life away from Cutler's Creek?

Away from her…

She wasn't the only person missing Ben, of course. Mike was looking downcast when JJ met him in the supermarket early on Sunday afternoon.

'We're all losing our fitness,' he told JJ. 'And getting rusty on important stuff like our abseiling skills. We've decided to do something about that. I might hike up Twin Rocks track later today and make sure it's not blocked by any trees or a slip or something.'

'Good for you.'

'So you're in, then? For a full session on Twin Rocks with the whole group next Saturday?'

'Oh, help…' JJ hadn't even been jogging

with Shaun in the last few weeks and she could remember only too well the pain of struggling up that track that first time. She had a whole week to get her body moving again before Saturday, though, and she couldn't encourage others without showing she was willing herself. The skills the guys in this community had when it came to difficult rescues were part of the legacy Ben had left a community he'd been passionate about. And it was a legacy more than well worth preserving. 'Okay… I'm in. Next Saturday.'

She would take Shaun out as soon as she got home, she decided. And, in the spirit of honouring Ben's legacy, she was also going to wear that old red, sweatshirt of his that he'd given her that day of the river crossing incident.

The day they'd first made love…

As a means of distracting herself, JJ couldn't wait to get started but it seemed that her pet sheep wasn't so enthusiastic and he was big enough now for it to be impossible for JJ to drag him into co-operating when he had no desire to go running.

'Oh, fine… I'll go by myself.' But, on the point of heading out to the roadside to start running, JJ changed her mind. If she was by herself, there was nothing stopping her from jumping into her car, driving to the start of the Twin Rocks track and giving that a go— just to find out whether she had, indeed, lost every bit of that fitness Ben had helped her achieve. The keys were still in her car, because Cutler's Creek was the kind of place where you didn't need to lock your car or house, so she didn't even need to take the time to go back into the cottage.

And it didn't matter that a quick glance at the sky revealed the slightly ominously dark bases to the huge, fluffy clouds. She wouldn't have to go all the way to the top to test her fitness level so she'd probably be home in an hour and back before Mike got started, which might be a good thing if she was out of breath and stopping too often. And, even if it did start raining before she got back home, it was no big deal. She wasn't going to melt, was she?

Halfway up the Twin Rocks track, JJ realised just how much harder this was after a few weeks of not pushing herself. She could even feel discomfort in that sprained ankle that had healed months ago. Instead of turning back, however, she pushed herself harder. Because she could imagine that Ben was watching her and, even if he couldn't possibly know about it, she still wanted to feel that he would be proud of her. The extra motivation worked well until she got to that point in the track where she had to scramble over those huge boulders. The ones that Ben had helped her negotiate that first time. How could she not remember what had happened only a little later that day. That moment when he'd been helping her into that harness. When the world had stopped turning for a heartbeat because they'd both been thinking about kissing each other.

And how much they'd wanted to…

The curl of desire was more like the stab of a knife in her belly and JJ knew she had tears streaming down her face. But she didn't stop. Or even slow down. She couldn't, because if she did, she might sit there sobbing, and how pathetic would that be? Ben had given her the gift of believing in herself and she was damned well going to make the most of it.

Maybe it was a burst of too much enthusiasm that did it. Perhaps it was because she was half-blinded by tears. It could have been that the first drops of rain had made the boulders more slippery than she remembered or, more likely, that she still had a residual weakness in the tendons of that ankle she'd sprained. Whatever the cause, the result was just as catastrophic. As she put every ounce of effort into boosting herself over the last obstacle, JJ lost her footing. She not only fell hard towards the downhill side of the track, she found herself rolling down the edge of the steep gully, through ferns and bracken and over hard lumps of rock.

It wasn't until she was caught by a larger rock nestled in the roots of a tree that the fall came to a crunching halt. She felt, rather than heard the snap of the bone in her ankle but she couldn't miss hearing the distant rumble of thunder that came in the next few seconds as she lay there, desperately trying to make sense of what had just happened and working out how badly injured she might be. The good news was that, apart from bumps and bruises, she didn't seem to have broken any other bones. The bad news was that JJ was realising just how many rules she had broken.

She wasn't dressed for bad weather.

She had no emergency supplies with her. She hadn't even brought her phone because she hadn't needed to go back into the cottage for her car keys.

She also hadn't told anyone where she was going or when she might return.

At the same time she was cataloguing her stupid errors, JJ had two other thoughts vying for prominence in the back of her mind.

One was how disappointed Ben would be in her.

The other was that she might well be in trouble, here.

Big trouble.

# CHAPTER TWELVE

'BIT OF BAD weather brewing down south. We might get grounded later on this afternoon.'

'Fine by me.' Ben waved at a stack of books on the table beside him. 'I've got a lot of revision to do. I've stuffed so much into my head in the last few weeks, some of it's in real danger of falling out.'

'Doubt that.' Phil, one of the air rescue base crew, grinned at him. 'You've aced your winch training. Your turn to dangle next time.'

'Maybe not today.' Ben looked through the windows of the rescue base's staffroom. 'I can see how fast those clouds are moving from here.'

A quieter spell on shift was welcome enough to make Ben wonder if the thrill of joining this crew might be wearing off just a little. Not that it wasn't as exciting as he'd dreamed it would be, it was just that you got used to anything, didn't you? He loved knowing that there was almost always a critically ill or injured patient waiting for them with every call and that the speed with which they could respond and the expertise they could bring to stabilising their patients made it very clear that lives were being saved.

But he did miss Cutler's Creek. He even missed having a callout to an old man who was a bit 'short of puff' due to his chronic lung disease rather than a severe asthma attack that had someone on the edge of a respiratory arrest. Because a case like Alfie was someone he knew? Part of a community that he'd also been a part of? He was missing Mike and Zac and all his other mates that he'd spent so much time training with. He was missing being near the mountains. And he was missing JJ a lot more than he'd expected, but wasn't that a warning signal that he'd left just in time? He'd never wanted an attachment that couldn't be broken voluntarily because that way, even if it got taken away from you, it wouldn't mean that you had to rebuild your whole life.

He was deep into a chapter of a manual covering winch techniques in difficult conditions and terrain when a call came in. The revision was forgotten as he listened to Phil on the radio. A mountain search and rescue team was asking for backup. Someone was missing in rugged country. A member of the team had found a car but its owner couldn't be located on the only track accessed from that parking area. With the weather closing in fast, they only had a small window of time to try and find the missing person before night fall and they needed help.

'Co-ordinates?'

Phil had their pilot beside him as he circled the area on the huge map behind glass on the wall. Ben was on his feet, as well. His mouth had gone dry as he saw the target area.

'That's Twin Rocks,' he said. 'Near Cutler's Creek.'

'You know it?'

'Like the back of my hand.'

Their pilot looked up from the screen where he was checking the latest weather information. He shared a rapid glance with Phil and the decision was made with a nod.

'Responding,' Phil told the control centre. 'Keep us informed. Any further details on who we're looking for would be helpful.'

'All we know so far is that it's one of the

local doctors. A woman in her thirties. Name of Hamilton.'

'*JJ...*'

The name came from Ben's lips in a horrified whisper but nobody else heard. They were all moving fast towards the helipad. In less than a minute they were airborne and on their way and they couldn't get there soon enough as far as Ben was concerned.

JJ could be hurt. Or worse…

And it made no difference that Ben had taken himself away. It wasn't going to make that particular loss any easier to live with. He'd thought he'd been in danger of falling in love with JJ. How blind had he been? It felt like his heart was already being ripped out here.

Because he already loved her.

He'd thought he could have lived his life knowing that she was safe and happy and with the type of person she would prefer to be with but he'd been wrong about that, too. He didn't want JJ to be with anyone else and…and he didn't believe that he could feel *so* sure of something if it was one-sided. If it was, he had to find out because living without JJ was always going to feel like living only half a life and, if it wasn't too late, he had to tell her that.

*Please...* he found himself repeating silently, with every air pocket that buffeted the aircraft as they sped towards the centre of the South Island. *Please don't let it be too late.*

They told her later that it was only thanks to that bright red sweatshirt she'd been wearing that they'd managed to spot her huddled between the rock and the tree on the side of that gully. And it had only been possible because they'd been circling Twin Rocks track with someone on board the aircraft who knew the area so well. Due to the distance she was from the track, the rain, the sound of wind in the trees and then the noise of the helicopter overhead, she hadn't heard any calls from the people on the ground who'd been searching for her and, even if she had, they wouldn't have heard her calling back.

They also told her she was lucky she hadn't been far more seriously injured or become more severely hypothermic given the amount of time she'd been missing, but it was all a bit of a blur for JJ. The fall had happened so fast and then she'd become cold very quickly and all she could really remember was the pain in her ankle that had made it impossible for her to move and try and save herself and how very, very scared that had made her feel. She'd huddled into that soft, red sweatshirt as it had begun raining harder and it had been another reminder of the last time she'd felt this scared—when she'd fallen in that river and the current had been threatening to sweep her away.

Perhaps that was why it had seemed like only a fantasy, through the blast of icy air and the roar of sound from the rotors above her, that the person inside that flight suit and hidden beneath the helmet and visor could be Ben Marshall. It wasn't until he'd unclipped himself and his equipment from the winch lines and had crouched right beside her that JJ had realised that she wasn't crazy. She really was about to be rescued and it really was Ben who was there to save her.

It didn't matter that he'd had to shout to make himself heard. He might as well have been whispering the words for her ears alone.

*'You're safe now,'* he'd told her. *'I've got you.'*

The pain relief Ben gave her before rapidly splinting her fractured ankle so that she could be moved without making the injury worse created a dreamlike edge to the drama unfolding around her that contributed to the blur that would come later. JJ had heard those words before, when she'd been pulled from that river and she had still been cold and shaking and frightened and yet she'd never felt so safe in her life—because she'd been in Ben's arms.

Another thought came from nowhere as he helped her into a harness. She'd known that somewhere along the line she'd fallen completely and utterly in love with Ben. Long before he'd told her how brave he thought she was. Had it been then—when he'd told her she was safe? When she'd *felt* so safe with him?

Like the way she did now?

When they were both clipped to that steel cable and JJ felt the moment they were in the air and being lifted towards the hovering helicopter, she knew that she'd never been in a situation quite this terrifying. There was still trust that she could cling to, however. She had Ben's arms around her again after all. He was with her as they flew to the large hospital in Dunedin. He stayed with her while she was assessed in the emergency department and his face was the last thing she saw before they put her to sleep in Theatre so they could operate on her ankle.

Ben's face was also the first thing she saw when she woke up and, despite everything—or perhaps because of everything—this felt like the happiest moment in her life. This was the face she wanted to see every time she woke up for the rest of her life, with that look in his eyes that told her how precious she was.

That she was loved *that* much…

He saw the instant her eyelashes flickered.

He saw the moment her eyes focused and she recognised who was sitting beside her bed. Holding her hand.

And he saw the way her whole face softened with an emotion that could only come from joy. Or love?

Hopefully both. A bucket of both.

'The surgery went really well,' he told JJ. 'You're doing really well. You just need to rest and recover now.'

'You're still here.' There was note of surprise in her whisper but Ben could see something else in her eyes. Hope…? He could feel his heart squeezing so hard and he just knew he'd been right. What he was feeling wasn't one-sided at all, was it?

'Why would I be anywhere else?' He tried to smile but this was too huge and he could hear the crack in his voice. 'I love you, JJ. Even if you do stupid things and break all the rules and nearly get yourself killed.'

Her eyes were trying to drift shut again but she was clearly determined to hold his gaze.

'I love you, too,' she murmured. Then her lips curved on one side. 'But I thought I wasn't your type.'

'I have a new type,' Ben said.

Her smile widened. 'Me, too.' One eye opened a crack. 'What's yours?'

'It's very exclusive.' Ben leaned closer. So close he could lean his head to touch hers. 'There's only one person in the world who could ever fill all the criteria.'

He could see the tiny wobble in JJ's lips. 'Sounds kind of like my new type.'

Ben had a bit of a lump in his own throat. 'Well…it does work, even if it shouldn't, doesn't it?'

'Mmm…' JJ's eyes were shut again. 'Okay…you'd better kiss me now. Before I fall asleep again.'

'Soon…' Ben had closed his own eyes. 'Very soon. I just want…*this* a little bit longer.'

Not that he needed any confirmation, but the fact that JJ didn't ask him what 'this' meant was proof that he'd found the person he was meant to be with. The way her hand tightened on his and kept holding it told him that she was feeling the same thing he was.

But he wanted to tell her anyway. Maybe he wanted to tell himself so that it became real. Soft words that were only intended for the two of them. JJ might think she'd dreamt them later but he could always tell her again.

'This is one of those moments, isn't it? When the world stops and there's this…stillness. When all you can feel is how much someone loves you. And how much you love them. *Where* you are doesn't matter. It's *who* you're with that's important.'

The soft sound JJ made was no more than a sigh but it was a sound of agreement. Of happiness.

'I had it when I was a little kid. With my Nana. When she hugged me. Or when we were together. Just us, and the rest of the world didn't matter. The fact that my mum never really wanted me didn't even matter.

It was…home. When she died, the bottom of my world fell out because I thought I'd never find that still place again. I didn't *want* to find it because I couldn't face how awful it was to lose it and so I keep moving, to make sure I *didn't* find it again.' Ben had to stop for a heartbeat, to swallow the lump in his throat. 'But there it was. When I was with you. In that time and that place that's just us. You and me.'

'Like this…?' JJ's head turned beneath his. She was still sleepy but she was listening to every word he was saying. Fighting to stay awake because she wanted to hear it all.

'Like this,' he agreed. 'But it scared me. Until something else scared me even more and that happened today, when I thought I might have lost you for ever. When I realised that living without you would only ever be living half a life.'

A single tear escaped JJ's eye and trickled down the side of her nose. 'I've missed you *so* much,' she murmured. 'I feel a lot braver when I know you're there.'

'And I need to know that I can go home,' Ben said. 'The world doesn't have to stop. I just need to know, deep down, that that still-ness is there. That I can go back to it as often as possible. Because it's where I need to be. The only place I ever want to be. It's…'

'Home,' JJ finished for him. 'It will always be there, Ben. For both of us. For as long as I'm alive, I promise.'

'And that will be for a lot longer if you can just learn to follow a few rules.'

JJ's lips were curling into a smile as he kissed her gently. And then he kissed her again. There would be plenty of time to talk about other things later. To plan the rest of their lives. Right now, he just needed to stay by the side of the woman he loved *this* much.

'Sleep now,' he whispered. 'You're safe. I'm not going anywhere.'

# EPILOGUE

*A few months later...*

THERE WAS ANOTHER one of Betty's legendary morning teas happening in Cutler's Creek Hospital's kitchen. It was becoming a bit of a local tradition that this was the place to make important community announcements and she was more than happy about that. It meant that she was always one of the first people to hear any news.

'This is absolutely going to be my last retirement speech,' Don Donaldson told everybody. 'And that's all I have to say on the matter.'

There was a ripple of laughter in the room.

'We'll see,' Bruce said. 'We all know you'll be back through that door in a heart-beat, Doc, as soon as you're needed.'

'And we wouldn't have it any other way.' Betty put another platter of savouries on the table—tiny potato-topped pies this time, which were one of her specialties. 'Babies, broken ankles, shortage of volunteers for the fire service or ambulance...whatever the problem, we've got it covered.' The solutions were often found during discussions that took place around this very table, a fact that Betty was rather proud of.

'My ankle's as good as new,' JJ said. She bounced on her toes to prove it. 'I got up Twin Rocks track the other day like it had never happened.'

'And there are no more babies on the way,' Liv added. 'Not from me, anyway. I've got more than enough on my hands as it is. Can someone please catch Hugo before he crawls out that door?'

It was Ben who swooped on the baby and then held him up high so that he shrieked with laughter.

'We shouldn't have any more shortages of volunteers for the ambulance either,' he assured the group. 'I'm starting a new training course next week now that I'm back here full time.'

'You're really giving up on the choppers?' Mike looked astonished. 'I thought you loved it.'

'I did. And I'm really grateful for all the extra skills I've picked up in the last few months but…you know…there are things I love even more than the excitement of that job.'

'Like Cutler's Creek.' Zac grinned. 'And all your frequent flyers like Albie and Bert.'

'Too right.' Ben nodded. But he had tucked baby Hugo against his hip and his gaze was on JJ. 'But that's not the only reason I'm back.'

A few knowing looks flashed around the kitchen but, for Betty, the feeling was one of relief. She didn't have to bite her lip any longer.

'Well…it's about time,' she said, with satisfaction. 'It's not as if we really believed that Dr Hamilton needed all those trips to Dunedin for physiotherapy on that ankle.' She was beaming as she peered over her glasses at Ben. 'Home is where the heart is, isn't that right, lad?'

'Oh, you have no idea how right you are, Betty.' Ben handed Hugo back to his mother and went to stand beside JJ. He put his arm around her shoulders and, as she looked up to meet his gaze, there was a soft sound in

the room, like a collective, happy sigh. Betty
was certainly a contributor.

'Seeing as you're all here and you've probably guessed anyway, we may as well tell
you that we're engaged.' Ben hadn't broken
that gaze yet. 'JJ accepted my proposal and
we're going to get married next month.'

'Here? In Cutler's Creek?' Betty had her
hands against her cheeks.

'Where else?' JJ was laughing. 'This is
where we met. Ben proposed to me up on
the top of Twin Rocks and we're not planning on living anywhere else. This is home.'

A delighted Liv turned to Don Donaldson.
'You never know, Dad. It might be a good
thing you've had some practice filling in for
people on parental leave.'

It was Ben and JJ's turn to exchange a
significant glance but, if there was a secret
there, they weren't ready to share it.

Not that it mattered. Betty was quite confident she'd be one of the very first to know
officially. Unofficially, she was quite confident she knew already.

These were two young people who obviously adored each other enough that being
together was all they needed but there was

something in that glance that suggested there was even more happiness to come.

It was contagious, that kind of happiness. Enough to make your heart melt, that's for sure. Betty had to reach for the corner of her apron to dry her eyes but she was already thinking of something else. Something important.

She had a wedding breakfast to plan…

\* \* \* \* \*

*If you enjoyed this story, check out these other great reads from Alison Roberts*

**A Surgeon with a Secret
A Pup to Rescue Their Hearts
Falling for the Secret Prince
The Paramedic's Unexpected Hero**

*All available now!*